SCIENTIFIC AMERICAN EXPLORES BIG IDEAS

How COVID-19 Changed the World

The Editors of *Scientific American*

SCIENTIFIC AMERICAN EDUCATIONAL PUBLISHING

New York

Published in 2023 by Scientific American Educational Publishing
in association with **The Rosen Publishing Group**
29 East 21st Street, New York, NY 10010

First Edition

Scientific American
Lisa Pallatroni: Project Editor

Rosen Publishing
Joseph Kampff: Compiling Editor
Michael Moy: Senior Graphic Designer

Cataloging-in-Publication Data
Names: Scientific American, inc.
Title: How COVID-19 changed the world / edited by the Editors of Scientific American.
Description: New York : Scientific American Educational Publishing, 2023. |
Series: Scientific American explores big ideas | Includes glossary and index.
Identifiers: ISBN 9781684169962 (pbk.) | ISBN 9781684169979
(library bound) | ISBN 9781684169986 (ebook)
Subjects: LCSH: COVID-19 (Disease)–Juvenile literature. |
Coronavirus infection–Juvenile literature. | COVID-19 (Disease)–Social
aspects–Juvenile literature. | Epidemics–Juvenile literature.
Classification: LCC RA644.C67 H69 2023 | DDC 362.1962'414–dc23

Manufactured in the United States of America

Cover: Corona Borealis Studio/Shutterstock.com
Websites listed were live at the time of publication.

CPSIA Compliance Information: Batch # SACS23. For Further Information contact
Rosen Publishing, New York, New York at 1-800-237-9932.

CONTENTS

INTRODUCTION

It's been more than two years since the beginning of the pandemic, and it's still difficult to say exactly what the ramifications of COVID-19 will be. What *is* clear is that the COVID-19 pandemic has had, and will continue to have, significant and lasting effects on the world in which we live. The reach of the COVID-19 pandemic extends far beyond the lives it affects due to illness, death, and the loss of loved ones. It has affected just about every facet of society.

The articles in this book not only document a changed world, they also bear witness to the world as it was changed by the pandemic. Some of the earlier articles, and even some of the more recent ones, were written at a time of great uncertainty. Section 1, "Setbacks and Advances in Science and Health Care," looks at the challenges and opportunities the pandemic presented to scientists and health care providers. While the pandemic was an unprecedented public health disaster in just about every regard, it stimulated enormous advances in the science of health care. Section 2, "The Pandemic Will Be Televised," addresses the ways information and misinformation about the pandemic circulated within the culture. Section 3, "COVID-19 and Society," provides insight into the ways COVID-19 reverberates in parts of society not immediately connected to health, such as how we conceive of work and the problems of economic disparity. Section 4, "Mental Health Crisis," looks at the tremendous effect the pandemic has had on mental health, perhaps most profoundly on children and young adults. Section 5, "The Aftermath of the Pandemic," presents an overview of the state of the world as the pandemic winds down. It appears that while the more immediate and devastating effects of the COVID-19 pandemic may be behind us, the reality of living in a post-pandemic world will be with us for a long time.

Section 1: Setbacks and Advances in Science and Health Care

A High-Speed Scientific Hive Mind Emerged from the COVID Pandemic

By Joseph Bak-Coleman and Carl T. Bergstrom

Most of the time science is a slow and tedious business. Researchers toil away for decades at obscure limits of human knowledge, collecting and analyzing data, refining theories, writing, debating, and advancing our understanding of the world in tiny increments. Working in small teams on highly specialized projects far from the public eye—that is what most of us are accustomed to doing.

But a calamity upends everything. In early 2020 COVID spread around the globe. Millions of lives were at stake. Yet we knew next to nothing about the nature of the threat. Just a few months earlier no one had ever seen the SARS-CoV-2 virus.

For researchers, the emergence of the disease was an all-hands-on-deck moment. Biologists such as the two of us, along with virologists and immunologists, all pivoted to focus on the new pathogen. And other researchers from across the scientific ecosystem—economists, physicists, engineers, statisticians, psychologists, sociologists, and more—dropped everything to learn about COVID and figure out how they could contribute. Public interest exploded. Scientists with scant experience in public communication learned to work closely with journalists, informing a worried public about what was happening, what to expect next, and what people could do to keep themselves safe. The scale of cooperation and collaboration is staggering. Large-scale surveys of scientists done in 2020 and 2021 show that roughly a third of researchers in the U.S. and Europe contributed to the effort.

This vast collaboration moved quickly and effectively in several areas. On December 30, 2019, an epidemiological surveillance network published the first English-language note about a cluster of pneumonia cases of unknown cause in Wuhan, China. Eight days later Chinese scientists identified the pathogen as a novel coronavirus. The full genome sequence was published just two days after that. Then on January 13, 2020, the World Health Organization published instructions for a PCR-based diagnostic test based on that genome.

The genome sequence also opened the door for vaccine development. Scientists used it to determine the 3-D structure of the SARS-CoV-2 spike protein, and by the end of January they had figured out how to stabilize the protein to make it an effective vaccine component, leading to mRNA-based and other vaccines, which were developed, tested, and distributed in less than a year.

The urgency of COVID drove scientists to adapt. Discussions that previously took place at conferences, on the telephone, or in revision notes on manuscripts moved to social media platforms such as Twitter, review sites such as PubPeer, and all-hours Zoom rooms. Researchers and clinicians spontaneously organized into focused teams and working groups. By rapidly sharing information on their patients, physicians figured out that people with severe COVID were at high risk for dangerous blood clots in their lungs, so anticoagulants became a standard of care and saved lives.

In general, traditional modes of publication were far too slow. We embraced a rapid alternative model: preprint archives, where papers are posted prior to peer review or consideration at a scientific journal. The number of papers submitted to medRxiv, a key repository of biomedical preprints, increased 10-fold in the first few months of the pandemic.

These changes also shifted early-stage science from a private activity to part of the public discourse. Instead of presenting the world with polished scientific articles, investigators worked in open view, thinking aloud, offering preliminary speculations, arguing, making wrong turns, following dead ends, and pursuing some hypotheses that would ultimately be refuted.

This approach to communication does have a downside. Previously private communications were now open to exploitation and distortion by politicians and pundits. For instance, flawed blood-sample research reported in an April 2020 medRxiv paper purported to show that COVID was a mild disease with a very low fatality rate. Although the scientific community quickly pointed out a host of problems with the work, people seeking to avoid business restrictions, school closures, and mask mandates ignored the criticism and used the paper to undermine public health interventions.

Rapid and unorthodox channels of communication also could not solve all the problems scientists encountered. We took too long to recognize the importance of airborne transmission of the virus. We spent early 2020 washing our groceries but not wearing masks. Most critically, we have been largely unsuccessful at anticipating and managing the human element of the pandemic. By not accounting for ways that behavior would change in response to information—and misinformation—we have struggled to predict the size and timing of successive disease waves and virus variants. A collective failure to stop misinformation from spreading on social and traditional media platforms has left large segments of the population unvaccinated, vulnerable, and unwilling to embrace measures such as masks and social distancing.

By some measures COVID has also hampered scientific productivity overall, researchers suggested in a paper in *Nature Communications* late last year. Some of the 2020 survey data revealed that scientists were spending an average of seven fewer hours per week working on research. The group, led by Dashun Wang of Northwestern University, wrote that the decrease in productivity will likely have lasting effects, with scientists reporting fewer publications, collaborations, submitted papers, and new projects started during the pandemic. Lockdowns, school closures, and other changes took a disproportionate toll on women scientists juggling work and child care—a major problem that requires urgent redress.

But a publication dip is precisely what we would expect when scientists shift from day-to-day research to an emergency response. Placing papers in journals becomes secondary to fixing problems. Dealing with urgent issues is one of the most important roles of the publicly funded scientific ecosystem, which has millions of researchers effectively on retainer. When global crises arise, they organize, learn, and coordinate. And that, ultimately, leads to solutions.

About the Authors

Joseph Bak-Coleman is a postdoctoral fellow at the University of Washington Center for an Informed Public. He studies how communications technology affects collective decision making.

Carl T. Bergstrom is a professor of biology at the University of Washington. He studies how evolution encodes information within genomes and how institutions and behavioral norms influence scientific communication.

The Pandemic Set Off a Boom in Diagnostics

By Roxanne Khamsi

A decade ago Willy Ssengooba began crisscrossing Uganda, training health-care workers on how to use a new machine to detect tuberculosis. The deadly lung disease infects around 90,000 people in the East African nation annually, but it can sometimes take months to diagnose using traditional methods such as culturing samples of coughed-up sputum. These new machines used rapid molecular testing to yield results within a couple of hours, meaning patients who tested positive could immediately be referred for lifesaving treatment. Ssengooba, who is scientific director of the mycobacteriology research unit at the Makerere University College of Health Sciences in Kampala, helped to set up 265 of the devices in clinics around the country. By increasing the number of early diagnoses—especially among vulnerable groups such as children and people living with HIV—deaths associated with tuberculosis dropped, too. Ssengooba saw this as a major success and wanted to deploy more machines. But it was hard to make politicians aware of the technology's power.

Then COVID arrived. Not long after the first case was reported in Uganda on March 21, 2020, Ssengooba received a message from a commissioner under the Ministry of Health. It had quickly become apparent that most of the new cases were coming through the border crossings, so screening people there would be a priority. Could Ssengooba make it possible to test everyone who wanted to enter Uganda? His entire country was counting on him.

Ssengooba and his team began facilitating the collection of nasal swabs taken from truckers at popular entry points, where imported goods are brought into the landlocked country. Those samples—sometimes more than 1,000 a day—then needed to be shuttled 150 miles to Kampala. The capital city was the nearest place with laboratory technology set up to run a process known as polymerase chain reaction–or PCR. Using fluorescent probes that latch onto portions of the coronavirus genetic sequence, these massive machines could determine whether a sample was positive for the genetic material of SARS-CoV-2.

Ssengooba's team had to shuttle the samples themselves. A crew of about 50 workers collected the samples in pickup trucks and delivered them to the lab, then turned around to go back for the next batch, spending long, exhausting nights on the road. As the pandemic intensified, they couldn't keep up. Truckers awaiting their test results were stalled at the border for days, in part because the sample analysis in Kampala would sometimes take up to 72 hours to return a result. A queue of trucks formed, stretching for kilometers, holding up the import of everything from home appliances to construction materials to replacement parts for cars. Making matters worse, authorities had closed the airport.

The government was desperate to alleviate the backlog. Ssengooba considered the 265 machines he had set up throughout Uganda over the years to test for tuberculosis. He realized he could repurpose some of those small PCR machines to test for the coronavirus by using a different sample-processing cartridge. He relocated that equipment directly to the border entry points and engineered some basic infrastructure (electrical power; benchtop safety spaces) to support their use. Unlike the lab setup in Kampala, which requires multiple machines spread across different rooms and experienced technicians to prepare and process the samples, these so-called GeneXpert modules were automated and about the size of a printer. They still used PCR technology but could return results on the spot in around half an hour.

By May the first COVID testing systems were working at the crossing point in the Kenya-Uganda border town of Malaba, reducing the waiting time for truck drivers from days to around half an hour. Within a week the equipment was set up at two other major border points. Many countries, even wealthy ones, struggled to get COVID screenings off the ground in the early months of the pandemic. But Ssengooba understood how to balance the needs of public health and the economy. By cobbling together testing infrastructure where it was most needed, he was preventing disease while keeping critical goods flowing into the country.

Ssengooba's creative repurposing of Uganda's limited testing resources was "tremendous," says Wilber Sabiiti, an expert at the University of St. Andrews in Scotland in the development of diagnostics tests. After Ssengooba had worked tirelessly for years to try to make PCR testing more accessible for tuberculosis, his efforts finally seemed to be getting validated. The pandemic, he says, has clarified the urgency of deploying PCR technology more widely for all kinds of infectious diseases, especially to politicians, who are now allocating more money to the technology. "The SARS-CoV-2 outbreak has been like a blessing in disguise for the scale-up of molecular assays," he says.

Ssengooba is hardly alone in his thinking. Alex Greninger, assistant director of the clinical virology labs at the University of Washington Medical Center, says that in the past, the facility where he works typically ran 50,000 PCR tests a year for diseases such as influenza and HIV. Between early 2020 and the end of 2021, it had done four million PCR tests, mainly for COVID. Unlike in the past, however, the results have been vital to informing immediate behaviors: those who test positive self-isolate or are kept in a special ward of a hospital. This has created a massive new reliance on testing to guide such decisions. "We [did] 81 years' worth of molecular testing in the virology lab in the first 22 months" of the pandemic, Greninger says. He expects the demand for PCR testing to stick around even after COVID ebbs. The general public is much more aware of virology now, he says, and as rapid antigen tests become a more routine part of living amid COVID and its potential future surges, people will seek out PCR tests to confirm positive results.

COVID has not just increased the scale of disease testing and created demand from pretty much everyone; it has also spurred the adoption of more advanced versions of the tests themselves. Hospital systems have begun purchasing PCR machines that are small enough to install at a doctor's office so that samples do not have to be sent offsite to a huge, centralized lab. That means patients can get a diagnosis on the spot and isolate immediately, if needed–and take whatever antiviral or antibiotic is most appropriate. Companies and university researchers around the globe who are working on PCR technologies say there is escalating interest in their innovations, such as handheld versions that would make testing anywhere–from supermarket parking lots to remote villages–more feasible.

All of this may benefit more than just individual patients. As the emergence of the quick-spreading Omicron variant demonstrated in late 2021, ramping up testing at the population level is crucial to keep tabs on how COVID might morph and push hospital systems (among other sectors of society) to a breaking point. The sweeping uptake of PCR for COVID could also pave the way for stronger public health surveillance systems that can spot future pandemics by scanning for dozens of pathogens at once. According to Jeffrey Townsend, a biostatistician at the Yale School of Public Health, PCR is a powerful tool to use for disease surveillance, and "there's a lot of people who say we need to be doing it even more."

A Strange Trip

In 1983 Kary Mullis was driving up to his cabin on the northern coast of California with his girlfriend, a chemist at the biotechnology company where they had been hired to synthesize genetic fragments. Mullis had spent earlier years completing a Ph.D. at the University of California, Berkeley, where he would trip on LSD while making new chemicals. His girlfriend had fallen asleep, and as he drove he had a vision of molecules dancing on the mountain road. It was then that the idea for polymerase chain reaction came to him. He pulled over the car and scribbled down his thoughts. It won him a Nobel Prize a decade later.

At its heart, PCR is a method of making copies of genetic sequences. There are now many dozens of different kinds of PCR, but the most basic form that Mullis devised started with a tiny bit of DNA and then used various cycles of heating and cooling to replicate it. First, the process would heat the DNA to break its double helix structure into two strands. Next, it would cycle to a cooler temperature that would allow specially tailored primers to bind to specific target sequences within the strands. The samples would be warmed up again, and enzymes would get to work building off those primers to finish replicating the complementary DNA sequences. The cycle would then repeat. Ultimately it yielded a lot of copies of the target strands. Special fluorescent tags were later added to the process to flag the presence of those amplified short sequences of interest.

It became possible to use this method to detect the presence or absence of pathogens: if a virus was present in a person's blood sample, for example, the PCR machine would make a lot of copies of its sequence, and the fluorescent tags would shine brightly. If there was no virus, there would be only darkness.

The incorporation of fluorescent tags meant that the PCR machines could also indicate how *much* virus was in a person's system. If the fluorescent light shined more strongly and sooner in the replication cycling, it meant more virus was present. A PCR could not only detect DNA, it could also detect genetic material known as RNA. This opened up a whole new world of diagnostics because many viruses, such as HIV, are RNA-based organisms. As the AIDS pandemic tore through the globe, doctors wanted to know *how much* HIV was circulating in their patients' bodies and whether the antiviral drugs they prescribed were working to keep the levels low. PCR could finally give them an answer.

The machines that did the analyses, though, required lab technicians with highly specialized expertise to prep samples and took half a day or more to return results. That changed after the U.S. Postal Service launched a competition for technology that could quickly screen mail for deadly anthrax spores, which a bioterrorist sent in letters to the offices of U.S. senators and journalists after 9/11. The winner, announced in 2002, was a GeneXpert prototype from Cepheid, a Silicon Valley diagnostics company founded in the late 1990s. The system automated many of the previously laborious sample preparation steps by using cartridges and valves that pull liquids through tiny channels and mix them together. And it returned results in minutes rather than hours. In the decades since, the GeneXpert platform has received approval to test for pathogens such as norovirus, chlamydia, tuberculosis, and SARS-CoV-2.

Cepheid says there are now more than 40,000 GeneXpert machines around the world, up from 23,000 in 2020. (The diagnostics branch of the major biomedical company Roche also has a PCR machine for clinics that is about the size of a coffee machine.) Increasingly, they are found at doctors' offices and at locations such as the border crossings in Uganda—rather than just at centralized labs. In September 2020 Cepheid received FDA authorization for a GeneXpert test that looks simultaneously for influenza A and B, SARS-CoV-2, and a pathogen that is particularly dangerous in young kids called respiratory syncytial virus. The test results, which can come back in about half an hour, help clinicians know what specific antiviral to give if a patient is sick—Tamiflu for influenza, for example, and Paxlovid for COVID. That is all the more crucial during a pandemic when your infection determines your isolation behavior.

Real-Time Warning Systems

It was not until the past decade or so that scientists established global surveillance systems that rapidly tracked outbreaks of viruses. Testing for pathogens fell to individual labs, and molecular diagnostics approaches such as PCR were expensive or unavailable. Furthermore, to do PCR testing for viruses of interest, scientists needed specific probes that would recognize a genetic sequence in the pathogens. But they lacked easy tools to create these probes. The barriers to conducting PCR and the dearth of repositories to upload such data made tracking the ebb and flow of viruses in populations spotty.

In 2012 the California Department of Public Health received several reports of a mysterious polio-like disease striking children. It manifested as a sudden onset of muscle weakness in the limbs, sometimes also leading to slurred speech and difficulty moving the eyes. The sick children did not have poliovirus, and health authorities ruled out other possible culprits, including West Nile virus, stroke, and botulism. What the children *did* have was an obscure virus called enterovirus D68, or EV-D68, which had first been identified decades ago. It had recently been linked with acute flaccid myelitis. Although some children make a full recovery from this condition, it can cause permanent paralysis and even death.

Around the same time that acute flaccid myelitis became associated with EV-D68, BioFire Diagnostics, a Utah-based molecular biology company that is now a subsidiary of the global diagnostics giant bioMérieux, began offering a comprehensive PCR-based respiratory test. It looked for 17 viruses and three bacteria in a single deep nasal swab taken from a patient.

Although the respiratory panel does not test specifically for EV-D68, it tests for the presence of the general family of viruses to which it belongs. BioFire wanted to find a way to catch EV-D68 outbreaks so that doctors and public health officials could know to keep patients from infecting others. Along with its academic partners, the company developed and tested an algorithm that was trained on past data to predict hotspots of EV-D68. The real proof of the approach came in 2018, when the algorithm alerted researchers to the emergence of EV-D68 that summer. Nationwide Children's Hospital in Columbus, Ohio, was one of the first places the algorithm identified with a possible uptick in cases of the virus; the team there confirmed the algorithm was right. As a result, the hospital implemented EV-D68 testing to catch cases early and prevent it from spreading.

A related surveillance platform that uses BioFire's PCR test collates data from different sites across the U.S. and other countries around the world on respiratory viruses such as influenza, rhinovirus, and now coronavirus, as well as more than a dozen gastrointestinal pathogens. Unlike the cumbersome data-collection protocols of the past, surveillance systems that continuously collect data directly from connected PCR machines have the potential to be used to detect outbreaks, including those of foodborne disease.

In many ways, this approach–combination PCR tests that cast a wider net to look for more possible pathogens in a given sample–signals the future of PCR. "Their instruments are phoning home, which is totally cool," Greninger says of the BioFire disease-tracking platform, explaining that the broad net it casts could help show where unexpected outbreaks are occurring. The COVID pandemic has made it clear that testing people for viruses even if they are asymptomatic can help identify those who would not otherwise know they are infected, prompting them to isolate before they pass the pathogen unknowingly to others in their community.

Viral evolution can sometimes create a challenge for PCR. Because the primers and probes used in the tests are tailored to look for specific, telltale sequences within a virus, sometimes a new viral variant can evade detection because its sequence has evolved beyond what the test is looking for. Test developers have to constantly ensure the primers and probes are up-to-date. "You need to have a very good understanding of emerging genomes in populations throughout the globe if you're going to have a globally applicable and accurate diagnostic PCR-based test," explains Alexandra Valsamakis, head of clinical development and medical affairs at Roche Diagnostics Solutions.

Yet once scientists have identified new viral variants, they can use PCR testing to track the spread of those variants. This is a capability that the antigen-based testing methods–which look for proteins unique to a particular pathogen–cannot do. The emergence of the Omicron variant has shown how vital it is to track variants. The data pouring in from PCR tests revealed that Omicron was spreading like wildfire compared with the Delta variant that preceded it. As a result, some governments began updating their guidelines and pushing for more booster shots, and some people took the data as a cue to reconsider their social interactions and upgrade the efficacy of their masks.

Some experts worry that even if PCR testing capacity expands to make more of this kind of surveillance possible, it will be hampered by insurance companies that might be unwilling to pay for asymptomatic testing or that hesitate to reimburse tests for pathogens for which no drugs or treatment are yet available. In most cases, insurance companies "pay for vaccines and diagnostics based on individual benefit," says Dan Wattendorf, the Innovative Technology Solutions team director at the Bill & Melinda Gates Foundation. "But we don't really have payment schemes or reimbursement and coverage to find transmission in the community." The problem with coverage for PCR testing has already been a sticking point in the coronavirus pandemic. The U.S. government set up requirements for health insurers to cover PCR testing for COVID, but consumers both with and without coverage have still been left with surprise bills in the thousands of dollars. Whereas PCR technology itself is undoubtedly powerful for disease surveillance, the question of who will foot the bill remains largely unanswered.

How COVID Is Shaping the Future of Diagnostics

As COVID created demand for more PCR testing everywhere, it also exposed how most of the technology relies on costly enzymes and single-use plastic parts for sample processing. After successfully setting up the fast-turnaround GeneXpert machines on Uganda's border in the spring of 2020, Ssengooba soon ran out of the cartridges and reagents the machines rely on. In those early months of the pandemic, Uganda requested 500,000 such cartridges from Cepheid, but Ssengooba says the company sent only 30,000. The test maker, he recalls, said that it was barred from sending more cartridges out of the U.S. "We spent the rest of 2020 without access to additional cartridges," Ssengooba says.

Modern PCR machines use plastic trays that traditionally have each contained 96 or 384 small wells to hold samples. To circumvent the need for expensive plastic "consumables" such as tubes and caps, U.K.-based company LGC replaces the tray with a long, flexible polymer tape. Only 0.3 millimeter thick, it can stretch up to 40 meters and has room for 106,368 reaction wells. "That allows you to do 100,000 to 150,000 tests per machine per day, which is 10 times more than any machine in the world at 10 times less cost," Wattendorf says, adding that the Gates foundation has partnered with LGC and Northwell Health, the largest health system in New York State, to try the tape-based method for COVID testing.

Another bottleneck with PCR is that "you have to get the sample very, very purified" before running the test, says biomedical engineer Nicholas Adams. PCR machines are calibrated to run reactions at specific temperatures, and impurities such as salts and proteins from patient samples and added preservatives can throw that off. Removing impurities is tough. To avoid that step, Adams and Frederick Haselton, both at Vanderbilt University, had the idea of adding DNA that is a mirror version of the target genetic sequence the PCR test is trying to detect. These mirror sequences are "left-handed"–meaning that they twist in the opposite direction of naturally occurring DNA, which is right-handed–so they do not interfere with the detection process. By adding a specific amount of the left-handed DNA and tracking how much of it is copied, Adams can use it as a benchmark to calibrate and confirm that the PCR machine is running without worrying about many impurities. Adams says that by reducing the need for purification with the left-handed DNA–which costs about 11 cents per test–labs could save significant labor and material costs.

Now that COVID has shown how important it is for testing to be accessible, there is more enthusiasm for portable PCR devices. Avleo Technologies has designed a handheld molecular testing machine that gives results in 30 minutes. Another device, from Visby Medical, was initially developed to look for sexually transmitted infections such as chlamydia and gonorrhea (and received FDA clearance for those applications) and has since added testing for SARS-CoV-2. Anavasi Diagnostics' AscencioDx platform, originally developed to detect HIV and flu before the pandemic hit, is being used in trials as a rapid molecular COVID test. In November 2021 the National Institutes of Health awarded $14.9 million to Anavasi to support that initiative.

Diagnostics developers are continuing to tinker with PCR. German engineering company Solarkiosk Solutions is developing a version that runs on solar power, which it is piloting for COVID testing in a remote part of Sumatra where many residents lack access to electricity and diagnostics. Academic labs and start-ups such as Mammoth Biosciences in San Francisco are combining traditional PCR methods with CRISPR gene-editing technology to make the tests more efficient at detecting specific pathogen genes.

At Uganda's border crossings, Ssengooba says that testing, at this moment, anyway, is "very smooth." But nearly 40 years after the idea of PCR was born, the technology is evolving rapidly as a result of the pandemic, and Ssengooba is dreaming big. He is eager to try the handheld disease diagnostics because traditional PCR—including the printer-size machines at the border—still require hookups to the electricity grid and various sample-processing rooms. A portable version, akin to the one in development by Indian company Molbio, could bypass some of these requirements and open up fast-testing access to remote areas for the first time. "This is something that is incredible," he says.

Public health has always been stymied by the hours or days between collecting a sample and delivering the results to the patient; in the meantime, an infected person has left the clinic and gone back to the routines of their life, unwittingly exposing others and delaying treatments that are often more effective if started earlier. COVID, and the stunning transmissibility of Omicron in particular, has laid bare the consequences of that gap—for individual health, community transmission, overburdened hospitals, labor shortages, and so much more. Ssengooba is hopeful that the urgency for closing that gap will persist. When imagining a future where portable PCR tests with on-site results are commonplace, "all of these challenges," he says, "are going to be left behind."

About the Author

Roxanne Khamsi is a science journalist and radio contributor based in Montreal. She has reported extensively on the COVID pandemic.

Mobile Clinics Can Help Reduce Health Inequity

By David E. Velasquez, LaShyra "Lash" Nolen, and Alister Martin

Grassroots organizers in Boston, primary care innovators in Chicago, and even an academic medical center in Philadelphia responded to the COVID pandemic by bringing mobile vaccine clinics directly to the neighborhoods most impacted by the virus. As a result, 85 percent of those vaccinated by Philadelphia's effort were Black, while 81 percent of those vaccinated by Boston's effort identified as persons of color. COVID mobile vaccine clinics work.

As the number of COVID cases falls in the United States, the frameworks used by mobile vaccine clinics should not be abandoned. Instead, these frameworks should be adopted and applied to health conditions that disproportionately impact communities of color. They provide health care delivery one path forward to achieving health equity.

One framework includes our own. Part of our team operates GOTVax, a grassroots organization in Boston that assembles providers, students, electoral campaign staff, and community organizations to upstand mobile vaccine clinics in communities of color. Our efforts leverage trusted community partners and get-out-the-vote tactics: wide-scale text messaging, phone banking, and door-knocking. So far, we have delivered over 6,000 vaccines to communities of color.

What would this framework look like with a health condition like hypertension, where 11 million people are undiagnosed and the burden of disease is disproportionately placed on patients of color?

First, the effort must include a wide-scale education campaign. Black people make up 13 percent of the U.S. population, but only about 5 percent of physicians are Black. This places many disadvantaged communities without trusted messengers in their vicinity to address health information deficits. This was especially a challenge with the COVID vaccines.

When the vaccines were first introduced in December, studies demonstrated that racial/ethnic concordance led Black patients to seek more information about the vaccine. However, historical instances of systemic racism, such as the Flexner Report, led to a paucity of Black physicians and left many Black community members without reliable resources to find information about the vaccine. Therefore, one of us created We Got Us, a nonprofit organization that connects Black community members and organizations with trusted Black health care personnel.

We Got Us holds empowerment sessions that engage community members in conversations about medical racism in Black communities, the vaccine development process, and specifics about the COVID-19 vaccines. Together, we increase access to the vaccine through a two-pronged approach by addressing both the informational and physical barriers to getting vaccinated.

Doing this work for hypertension could mean that discussions revolve around medical racism in communities of color, the drug development process for common hypertensive drugs, and specifics about the disease. Research shows that individuals with higher general trust in the medical system are more likely to report better adherence to hypertensive medications. Further, the signs and symptoms of hypertension are often misunderstood. Deploying community-specific education programs will be critical to ensuring health equity.

Second, the effort should deploy a tactical canvassing approach to ensure that identified community members are being targeted for education and clinic day purposes. At GOTVax, we conduct three rounds of outreach: text messaging, phone banking, and door-canvassing. To reach community members untouched by our health care system—typically Black and Latinx folks—we work with public housing managers, unions, and community-based organizations. Through them and our on-the-ground door knocking volunteers, we are able to develop outreach lists that are used to sign people up for the COVID-19 vaccine.

Operationalizing this strategy for hypertension would be similar to our approach. Outreach workers would text, call, and have face-to-face conversations with individuals. If the recipient has not been screened for hypertension, they would be made aware of an upcoming hypertension clinic. If the recipient has hypertension but adds that their condition has not been consistently managed, they would also be invited to the clinic. Those with a diagnosis and adequate treatment would require no further follow-up.

Similar to the GOTVax approach, this outreach operation should include multilingual, multiracial, and multiethnic workers. Research shows that Black people are more likely to receive preventive services when seeing a Black doctor, as opposed to a non-Black doctor. The same is likely true for other communities of color.

The final piece of the framework includes hypertargeted clinics. After education and outreach, we set up clinics in communities with poor access to vaccination centers. Hypertension clinics could take place in gymnasiums, churches, public housing units, and other community spaces within disadvantaged communities. They could also be aided by local community health vans that already operate within these neighborhoods, such as the Family Van in Massachusetts.

Individuals would be signed up for an appointment during outreach and the appointment could include hypertension screening, medication reconciliation, signing up eligible patients for health insurance, and connecting patients with a primary care provider.

Transitioning from a vaccine-focused campaign to campaigns focused on other health conditions will require input from various stakeholders, from those we work with (electoral campaign staff, community organizations, etc.) to new partners such as physician subspecialists. They will also need to be well-resourced and should consider partnering with a community health center or academic medical center committed to communities of color.

There will likely be much iteration of these efforts, given their infancy and novelty. We at GOTVax and We Got Us have learned from our experience and applied lessons appropriately. As a result, we have noticed the impact that intentional, hypertargeted mobile clinics and health education have on the populations most impacted by COVID. Upstanding clinics for other medical conditions will likely have a similar impact and bring us one step closer to the health equity we deserve.

About the Authors

David E. Velasquez is a medical student at Harvard Medical School and a member of GOTVax.

LaShyra "Lash" Nolen is a medical student at Harvard Medical School and the founding executive director of the We Got Us empowerment project.

Alister Martin is an emergency room physician and founder of GOTVax.

COVID Revealed the Fragility of American Public Health

By Wendy E. Parmet

Epidemics expose a society's vulnerabilities. And we were already an unhealthy population before COVID emerged. Compared with some other developed countries, the U.S. has extraordinary rates of chronic obstructive pulmonary disease, diabetes, and other afflictions that leave people more susceptible to severe COVID. These vulnerabilities were influenced strongly by social factors—not purely genetics.

How did we get here? Partially it was because our public health system had been depleted and eroded. Public health has long been the second-class cousin of the individual health-care system, even though they are closely related. In recent history, we spent lots of money on individual treatment and invested far less in *population* health. Public health systems lacked adequate personnel, data systems for analysis, the latest technology, and government support.

Adding to an already perilous situation, the pandemic exposed and accelerated preexisting trends in our society, such as growing distrust of institutions, including of science. In the past 20 years or more American conservatism transformed to antiscience populism. Even in the legal sphere, there has been a dramatic change in the past year in how many courts, including the U.S. Supreme Court, look at public health—a shift from perhaps being excessively deferential to public health policies to becoming hostile to public health, embracing an antiregulatory approach that spans various doctrinal categories.

With such a great push toward individualism, populism, and a judicial review that is skeptical of public health, how do we keep the gains we've made against childhood diseases such as polio and measles, chronic illnesses such as those caused by smoking, and motor vehicle accidents? Life expectancy climbed in the 20th century not only because of tremendous scientific advancements and increasing wealth but also because public health campaigns and public health laws accomplished a lot. In the backlash against COVID restrictions and policy, we risk undoing all that.

About the Author

Wendy E. Parmet is the Matthews Distinguished University Professor of Law and a professor of public policy and urban affairs at Northeastern University.

How COVID Changed Science

By William A. Haseltine

Rarely in recent memory has the world faced such an immediate and widespread global threat as complex as COVID-19. In its face, a select few have risen to the occasion, none more cherished and admired perhaps than the health care workers staffing the front lines. But standing close behind them in the trenches are the scientists and researchers who are among the very few who truly understand the scope of our evolutionary battle with the virus. Since the start of the pandemic, our scientists have acted with unprecedented speed and coordinated action to deliver us an armamentarium of medical weaponry to confront this global threat.

For someone who has spent a lifetime in science, someone who understands the pressures and constraints faced each day in every lab, it has been phenomenal to witness the transformation that has taken place within the scientific community. It is not just the speed and focus with which the scientific community responded, nor simply the use of new technologies to draw out new discoveries, but rather the singular willingness of scientists, all over the world, to share new ideas and data immediately and transparently, in some cases well before the idea or the research is fully formed.

Within weeks of the first case of COVID being reported, Chinese researchers had identified the virus they suspected of causing the disease and had decoded an initial genome sequence. It was a remarkable achievement in such a short amount of time, made more remarkable by the fact that the researchers published the sequence in an open discussion forum online, and encouraged a fellow researcher in Sydney, Australia, to share it via Twitter with the world.

During the first 24 hours after publication, an evolutionary biologist in Scotland had figured out the similarities between this virus and SARS-CoV-1 and, like the Chinese researchers, shared the findings immediately online. A researcher in the U.S. openly published the new virus' phylogenetic tree. And another started reverse-engineering a live virus from the sequence, letting colleagues around the world know that the first steps towards developing an antibody test were already underway. At each moment, the goal was not acclaim or attention, but rather the possibility that openly sharing an early finding may influence the work of others and inch the world ever closer to a treatment or a cure.

Of all the arenas in life that COVID has upended, science is perhaps the field that has been transformed the most. The pandemic has created an entirely new research environment, one that is now structured for collaboration and communication above all else. This revolution was inspired by the initial transparency of those early researchers but has since been institutionalized by some of the most well-respected research institutes in the world today, including our very own biomedical nerve center in Boston.

Shortly after the virus emerged, Harvard Medical School pulled 20 Boston-area universities, medical schools, and research institutes together to launch the Massachusetts Consortium on Pathogen Readiness (MassCPR). The initial goal was to formally join forces with researchers in China to answer the call to action to take down the emerging threat, with the hope that any lessons learned from this outbreak would enable a more rapid response to future emergencies.

This alone was a notable step. The scientific community in Boston typically works in relatively isolated fashion, with barriers built up between departments, disciplines, and entire institutions. But with COVID-19 and MassCPR those floodgates between institutes upriver and down were quickly opened.

With a collaborative research grant from the Evergrande Group, MassCPR began funding dozens of new research projects, some of which have led to field-defining studies on the epidemiology, pathogenesis, and immunopathology of COVID-19. Over the past year, MassCPR clinicians have written clinical management guidelines that have influenced patient care across the globe, and the consortium's investigators have conceptualized, designed, and developed the single-dose Johnson & Johnson vaccine and spearheaded clinical trials for the Moderna one.

The dean of Harvard Medical School, George Daley, leads the effort, along with Arlene Sharpe, Bruce Walker, and David Golan. As Daley describes it, "Our collective efforts over the last year have given us demonstrable proof that we are strongest when we work together across institutional boundaries, when we reach out across geographic and national borders. We are strongest when we transcend scientific silos and build bridges across disciplines. Cooperation to confront a common threat is what MassCPR represents, and the achievements speak for themselves."

MassCPR's immediate efforts are focused on the basic biology of SARS-CoV-2 and the pathogenesis of COVID-19—developing new diagnostic tools, vaccines, and therapies. But while the researchers stay firmly focused on the now, they are also looking towards tomorrow. "We must refine our capacity to track the rise of new viral variants," warns Daley. "We must refine our prevention strategies—an armamentarium of treatments—by developing new antiviral drugs, panviral therapies, and polivariant vaccines. And we must anticipate the post pandemic realities of COVID-19. A major goal of MassCPR 2.0 will be to define the scope of post-COVID-19 syndrome and understand the long-term effects of multiple organ systems. The knowledge will have relevance beyond this pandemic and, indeed, beyond this pathogen."

Beyond MassCPR, other critical global partnerships have emerged over the course of the past year to bring recent scientific advancements on the virus to the masses, not the least of which is the Access to COVID-19 Tools (ACT) Accelerator and its vaccines pillar, COVAX. The ACT Accelerator is a global philanthropic partnership—not a new agency or institution but rather a framework for collaboration launched by the WHO, the European Commission, France, and the Bill & Melinda Gates Foundation in April 2020.

ACT is focused on accelerating the development and production of COVID-19 tests, treatments, and vaccines (via COVAX) and, perhaps most critically, on ensuring that all people, and all countries, can access and afford these miracles of science. While richer countries have been able to roll out vaccines at no cost to residents, lower-income countries are still struggling to determine how to procure and pay for the vaccines in the first place, much less distribute them fairly across their countries. Rough estimates suggest that it would cost around $30 billion to mass-vaccinate the world—a price rich countries may not choose to shoulder. Take for example the United States, whose portion of the cost to help vaccinate the world is $7 billion. That figure is less than 0.5 percent of what was approved as part of the March 2021 economic stimulus package, mere pennies in relative terms but critical to ending the pandemic.

Global fundraising for health is by no means without precedent, but what makes the ACT Accelerator unique is the burden-sharing formula it proposes to generate the funds. Every country is given a recommended range to contribute, which is adjusted based on GDP and the size of the country itself. The goal is to create a fair and equitable framework to respond to this crisis and future emergencies, including other pandemics—a systematic plan to prevent any country from having to choose again between who lives and who dies.

This collective solution to the problem at hand also has scientists in the lead, with researchers monitoring the vaccine landscape and advising COVAX on the most suitable candidates based on scientific merit and scalability and with major pharmaceutical companies committing to providing hundreds of millions of doses—eventually billions—to distribute around the world. Scientists have not only worked together to develop COVID treatments and vaccines, but they are among the loudest voices calling for rich countries to collaborate and to deploy their wealth across all countries to end the disease.

Yet even with these remarkable scientific efforts, there is perhaps no better indicator of the extent to which the scientific community is focused on collaboration than by how entirely the scientific publication process has been upended. Publication in a well-respected journal is a competitive and highly prized honor, considered so by even the most accomplished scientists. Whereas in the past, researchers were willing to wait months and sometimes more than a year for the distinction, those imperatives have since been set aside. Researchers now proactively share preprint versions of their studies immediately after they determine their results, not only for recognition but in the hopes that their discoveries will help other scientists further their own. Between the start of the pandemic in December 2019 and November 2020, around 75,000 scientific papers were published on COVID-19, with one-third published as preprints, released to other scientists and the public at large, before being fully reviewed and accepted for journal publication.

As scientists choose to forgo some of the academic recognition that comes with waiting for traditional publication, the journals themselves have shifted their approach as well, rethinking work flows to publish COVID-related papers much faster than normal. Yet this has not been without consequence. In the spring of 2020, two COVID studies were famously retracted over concerns about the veracity of the primary data. Some journals have admitted they may need to slow the process down again to ensure the quality of the work. Still, the knowledge gained has arguably outweighed the risks, given that the rapid advancements on vaccines, treatments, and our understanding of the disease are owed in large part to the immediate and transparent release of new data.

The question still remains whether this sense of shared purpose and transparent cooperation is a temporary measure or the beginning of a new era of scientific collaboration and global partnership. I can't help but hope that this is indeed the beginnings of a new milestone in human achievement. Science is a tradition built on thousands of years of incremental progress. Imagine the exponential increase if our collaborative efforts continued–a global community united against the most pressing economic, social, and environmental problems of our time.

As Daley of the Harvard Medical School and MassCPR put it, "I cannot help but think that [it] provides a blueprint for moonshot projects that bring together the strongest and most dynamic forces of our formidable, biomedical ecosystem. What if we could marshal these forces against future pandemics, other diseases, and larger global challenges? I dare to imagine the possibilities."

With all the tragedy of the past year and the losses we have suffered, this revolution in the scientific community and beyond may be the one exquisite thing to emerge.

About the Author

William A. Haseltine is a former Harvard Medical School professor and founder of the university's cancer and HIV/AIDS research departments. He also serves as chair and president of the global health think tank ACCESS Health International. He has founded more than a dozen biotechnology companies and is the author, most recently, of Variants! The Shape-Shifting Challenge of COVID-19.

Section 2: The Pandemic Will Be Televised

The Lab-Leak Theory of COVID's Origin Is Not Totally Irrational

By Naomi Oreskes

In June a well-known climate scientist opined on Twitter that "I'd be more likely to believe the COVID lab-leak hypothesis if the people pushing it weren't largely the same people pushing [bogus] conspiracy theories about the 2020 presidential election and climate change." He has a point. Early in the pandemic, the lab-leak theory was promoted by then president Donald Trump, who was dismissive of masks and social distancing. He speculated that COVID-19 infections might be effectively treated by irradiating sensitive lung tissues with ultraviolet light, using untested and possibly unsafe drugs, or injecting dangerous household cleansers. Trump also knowingly put his own Secret Service detail at risk by riding with them in a closed car while he was fighting an active infection, misrepresented hurricane forecasts, and advanced misleading ideas about vaccine safety. And–most egregiously for climate scientists–he repeated the ridiculous claim that climate change was a hoax.

We all judge messages by the messenger. If our trust (or lack of it) is grounded in experience, this pattern is rational: we would be foolish to trust someone who in the past has repeatedly misled us, been mistaken, or given us bad advice. We wouldn't go back to a doctor who had misdiagnosed a serious disease or a car mechanic who had cheated us. We wouldn't stick with a financial adviser whose stock tips had consistently proved wrong.

To be clear, most scientists think animal spillover is the most likely explanation because that's where most new diseases come from. True, the source animal has not yet been identified, but it took decades to determine that HIV was derived from primates. True, there is a lab in Wuhan that studies bat viruses, but it's typical for scientists to study viruses endemic to their regions. And blaming humans for disease is as old as disease itself.

But what do we do when evidence suggests that a claim might be right, even if the person making it has been repeatedly wrong? Here it's helpful to distinguish between two forms of the lab-leak theory: the malevolent and the accidental. The malevolent version holds that China deliberately released the virus. I know of no credible scientists who embrace that idea, and it strikes me as unlikely because politicians with even the most meager understanding of pandemics would realize that any deliberately released virus would affect China as much as or more than the countries to which they hoped to spread it.

The accidental version holds that the virus got out by mistake. Here things get trickier but more plausible. Even institutions that take great safety precautions still sometimes fail. Just think about the nuclear power industry, where serious accidents have occurred in Japan, the Soviet Union, the U.K., the U.S., Canada, France, Belgium, Sweden, and Argentina and minor or moderate accidents in most countries where nuclear power is used. Or consider railroads, where major accidents still occur every year; the most deadly accident in U.S. railroad history occurred in Tennessee in 1918, almost 100 years after the industry got started.

The late Yale University sociologist Charles Perrow developed the theory of "normal accidents" to explain this phenomenon. People are human. We all make mistakes. Fortunately, our mistakes are often minor and can be easily corrected. But in complex technological systems, small mistakes may rapidly ramify and compound into large problems. When people don't know how to fix their mistakes–and are perhaps embarrassed or ashamed–they may try to cover them up, impeding the ability of those around them to fix the problem, too.

It's not hard to imagine that a COVID researcher made a small mistake and tried to hide it, and things then spiraled out of control. It doesn't mean this is what happened, but it does mean we should keep an open mind until we know more. The lab-leak theory is plausible, and it is rational for scientific institutions to investigate closely, even if some of the people promoting the claim are irrational.

Life is short, research is expensive, and not every theory is worth pursuing. But when the stakes are high, it generally behooves scientists to look closely at any idea that has not yet been properly evaluated. If there is credible evidence that the SARS-CoV-2 virus may have escaped from a lab–in China or anywhere else–that evidence should be evaluated, even if we first heard the message from an untrustworthy messenger.

About the Author

Naomi Oreskes is a professor of the history of science at Harvard University. She is the author of Why Trust Science? *(Princeton University Press, 2019) and co-author of* Discerning Experts *(University of Chicago, 2019).*

A Grassroots Effort to Fight Misinformation During the Pandemic

By Lindsay Milliken, Michael A. Fisher, and Ali Nouri

During the height of the deadly COVID-19 pandemic, with misinformation permeating every form of media, members of the public were growing increasingly concerned for their health and seeking answers about the virus, its mode of transmission, and how to protect themselves and their loved ones. Five organizations came together, recruited hundreds of volunteer scientists, and built a new tool to get the best scientific information in plain language to millions of people around the world. This is the story of that project.

In March, with the help of other organizations, the Federation of American Scientists (FAS) launched Ask a Scientist to enable the public to literally ask a scientist any question related to SARS-CoV-2. The site is loaded with information from reputable scientific and public health sources such that it recognizes questions and provides an automated response. But for more custom-made questions, the public can send an email to a network of hundreds of scientists and get a response back in their inbox.

Throughout the pandemic, the site was viewed by millions of users as our expert volunteers, made up of graduate students, postdoctoral fellows, and faculty members, answered thousands of questions, making Ask a Scientist one of the go-to resources online. What began as a small project to combat rampant misinformation about the pandemic quickly grew into a large effort that brought together experts in virology, medicine, public health, and more to help the public access up-to-date information.

In the Beginning

In early February, news of the spread of a novel and deadly coronavirus had the U.S., and the world, on edge. Social media was rife with conspiracy theories and misinformation regarding the virus' origin, how it spreads, and its severity. FAS, whose mission in part is to connect scientists with policy makers and the public, formed a small group of researchers to tackle this misinformation. The group collected and analyzed the most pervasive myths surrounding SARS-CoV-2, and then used sound reports and the scientific literature to debunk them.

We then launched a Web site to bring the up-to-date information to the public. It included answers to commonly asked questions and also catchy and simple PSAs on how to best protect oneself and loved ones. We also pushed out this information on social media. We included ways for the public to interact with our researchers to get their questions answered.

Soon after, news of our efforts spread in media outlets, on social media, and by word of mouth. Our researchers were flooded by queries from a hungry public and the demand was far bigger than our small team at FAS could handle.

Enter NYU and New Jersey

The solution was simple: if you can't handle the incoming volume of questions, build a Web site that can automatically answer them. So FAS partnered with the New York University GovLab and the State of New Jersey Office of Innovation to build an entirely new Web site to make it easier to find answers to the most pressing questions about COVID-19, and rebranded the project as Ask a Scientist.

We preloaded the site with answers to hundreds of questions researched by us, or taken directly from the CDC, the WHO, and other established public health entities. This new Web site also contained an answer-bot that automatically loads answers to questions typed in the search bar. Users can go in-depth, read about tangentially relevant issues, and even share each answer onto social media. Additionally, through a partnership with Amazon, we enabled users to interact with the site through their Alexa home device.

Ask a Scientist

Notably, we added a feature to the site allowing those who did not find an answer to their question to send us a question and receive a response. But this time we were ready for the deluge, thanks to a partnership with the National Science Policy Network, an organization of hundreds of graduate students and postdocs aiming to promote the involvement and impact of early-career scientists and engineers in public policy.

This diverse group of scientists looking to make a difference during the pandemic was critical to the project's success because they could field questions quickly and respond to a concerned public. By March 15, the Ask a Scientist volunteer network contained 150 graduate students (140 Ph.D. candidates and 10 master's students), 100 Ph.D.s, 18 medical doctors, 50 with degrees in public health, 30 in virology, 30 in immunology, 20 in epidemiology, and 15 with expertise in science, health, or risk communication. Interest in the project only increased from this point forward, and a skilled editing team was recruited to ensure all of Ask a Scientist's answers passed strict quality control measures.

To increase Ask a Scientist's ability to reach as many members of the public as possible, the project's Web site was translated into Spanish by a dedicated team of bilingual scientists. By the end of May, Ask a Scientist partnered with hundreds of NSPN members with expertise in virology, epidemiology, and public health, as well as scientists from leading institutions who wanted to give back to their communities as the virus spread throughout the U.S.

Answers crafted by Ask a Scientist's team of experts were also appraised for their value to others and, after removing any personally identifying information, were vetted by senior, Ph.D.-level scientists and made publicly available in the initiative's comprehensive knowledge base. By doing this, the Ask a Scientist "answer bot" continued to get smarter and smarter. These answers were frequently updated to provide an easy-to-navigate database of information about the COVID-19 pandemic for the general public.

By mid-April, Ask a Scientist was featured on the National Governors Association's Web site as a resource for state and local officials during the COVID-19 pandemic, as well as embedded in the New Jersey and Alabama state government Web sites where it was being viewed by millions on a weekly basis. In an April press conference, New Jersey Governor Phil Murphy called Ask a Scientist a "truly unique feature" that helps people get the answers they need to protect their families; he noted there had already been over two million visits to the New Jersey site at that point.

Ask a Scientist expanded so quickly that it outgrew its original organizational structure. Questions flooded in from the public and the number of volunteer scientists swelled to over 500. The team reached out to Accenture to help build a completely new back-end system to categorize and respond to questions. Both groups collaborated closely to construct a portal for the volunteers to make it easier to sort, answer, and edit responses for the public, as well as communicate with each other to ensure that volunteers answered questions that aligned with their expertise. Ask a Scientist also grew in popularity in other countries. Our team received questions from 10 foreign nations, including Russia, India, Italy, the United Kingdom, New Zealand, France, Canada, Switzerland, Germany, and Spain.

A New Phase

By May, the Ask a Scientist project had grown to not only provide the public with sound information, but also inform policy makers. The new initiative, called the COVID-19 Rapid Response Task Force, is based on a similar notion: crowdsource expertise from those who work across U.S. research institutions to inform the work of policy makers. To do this, FAS gathered some of the brightest scientific minds, in subjects such as virology, testing, big data, public health, treatments and vaccines, supply chain management, infectious disease medicine, and international public health policy, to provide the best information as quickly as possible to federal and state lawmakers.

LOOKING AHEAD

Ask a Scientist has been an effort of collaborative science policy and communication, as experts from all over the world worked together to translate cutting-edge research for the public and deliver the most accurate advice. It is an effort to combat misinformation and provide individuals with the information they need in their everyday lives. This pandemic has clearly shown that effective science communication is essential to keep people safe. Collaborative, grassroots initiatives like Ask a Scientist can make a real impact in these efforts.

About the Authors

Lindsay Milliken is a research assistant for science, technology, and information policy at the Federation of American Scientists. She supports both the Congressional Science Policy Initiative and the Technology and Innovation Initiative.

Michael A. Fisher, Ph.D., is a senior fellow with the Federation of American Scientists, working on a range of issues across the science and technology policy landscape. He co-leads the Congressional Science Policy Initiative, coordinates the COVID-19 Rapid Response Task Force and is a member of its steering committee, and works on the Ask a Scientist and Coronavirus Project teams.

Ali Nouri, Ph.D., a molecular biologist, is the president of the Federation of American Scientists. Nouri is co-chair of the National Academies of Sciences, Engineering, and Medicine's New Voices Initiative, and serves on the academy's Global Diplomacy Roundtable. He previously served as a biotechnology adviser in the office of the UN Secretary General and served nearly 10 years as a senior adviser and legislative director in the U.S. Senate.

To Understand How Science Denial Works, Look to History

By Naomi Oreskes

2020 has been a historic year–and mostly not in a good way. Among many things, we saw a historic level of disregard of scientific advice with respect to the COVID-19 virus, a disregard that made the pandemic worse in the U.S. than in many other countries. But while the events of 2020 may feel unprecedented, the social pattern of rejecting scientific evidence did not suddenly appear this year. There was never any good scientific reason for rejecting the expert advice on COVID, just as there has never been any good scientific reason for doubting that humans evolved, that vaccines save lives, and that greenhouse gases are driving disruptive climate change. To understand the social pattern of rejecting scientific findings and expert advice, we need to look beyond science to history, which tells us that many of the various forms of the rejection of expert evidence and the promotion of disinformation have roots in the history of tobacco.

Throughout the first half of the 20th century, most Americans saw science as something that made our lives better. Science had deepened our understanding of the natural world, which helped us to cure diseases, light our homes, and bring new forms of entertainment into our lives. Perhaps most important, physicists helped to win World War II and became cultural heroes. Chemists got their due, too. As DuPont reminded us, we had "better things for better living through chemistry." At General Electric, scientists and engineers were helping to "bring good things to life." These were not just slogans; corporate R&D really did produce products that measurably improved many American lives. But corporate America was also developing the playbook for science denial and disinformation.

The chief culprit in this darker story was the tobacco industry, whose playbook has been well documented by historians of science, technology, and medicine, as well as epidemiologists and lawyers. It disparaged science by promoting the idea that the link between tobacco use and lung cancer and other diseases was uncertain or incomplete and that the attempt to regulate it was a threat to American freedom. The industry made products more addictive by increasing their nicotine content while publicly denying that nicotine was addictive. With these tactics, the industry was able to delay effective measures to discourage smoking long after the scientific evidence of its harms was clear. In our 2010 book, *Merchants of Doubt*, Erik M. Conway and I showed how the same arguments were used to delay action on acid rain, the ozone hole, and climate change–and this year we saw the spurious "freedom" argument being used to disparage mask wearing.

We also saw the tobacco strategy seeping into social media, which influences public opinion and which many people feel needs to be subject to greater scrutiny and perhaps government regulation. In October 2019 Congress held hearings to investigate the role of Facebook in potentially spreading misinformation. In the summer of 2020 a report from civil-rights law firm Relman Colfax suggested that Facebook posts could contribute to voter suppression. Climate scientists have complained that the social media giant contributes to the spread of climate denial by permitting false or misleading claims while hobbling responses by mainstream scientists by labeling their posts "political."

Without a historical perspective, we might interpret this as a novel problem created by a novel technology. But this past September, a former Facebook manager testified in Congress that the company "took a page from Big Tobacco's playbook, working to make our offering addictive," saying that Facebook was determined to make people addicted to its products while publicly using the euphemism of increasing "engagement." Like the tobacco industry, social media companies sold us a toxic product while insisting that it was simply giving consumers what they wanted.

Scientific colleagues often ask me why I traded a career in science for a career in history. History, for some of them, is just "dwelling on the past." But, as the bard said in *The Tempest*: "What's past is prologue." If we are to confront disinformation, the rejection of scientific findings, and the negative uses of technology, we have to understand the past that has brought us to this point."

About the Author

Naomi Oreskes is a professor of the history of science at Harvard University. She is the author of Why Trust Science? *(Princeton University Press, 2019) and co-author of* Discerning Experts *(University of Chicago, 2019).*

Making Vaccines Is Straightforward; Getting People to Take Them Isn't

By Naomi Oreskes

There is a saying in the field of artificial intelligence: "Hard things are easy; easy things are hard." Called Moravec's paradox, after Hans Moravec, founder of robotics company Seegrid, it is explained in detail in a recent book by computer science professor Melanie Mitchell entitled *Artificial Intelligence: A Guide for Thinking Humans*. Activities that most people find very hard, such as playing chess or doing higher mathematics, have yielded fairly readily to computation, yet many tasks that humans find easy or even trivial resist being conquered by machines.

Twenty-five years ago Garry Kasparov became the first world chess champion to lose to a computer. Today computer programs can beat the world's best players at poker and Go, write music, and even pass the famous Turing test–fooling people into thinking they are talking to another human. Yet computers still struggle to do things most of us find easy, such as learning to speak our native tongue or predicting from body language whether a pedestrian is about to cross the street–something that human drivers do subconsciously but that can stymie even the most advanced self-driving cars.

AI researchers will tell you that chess turned out to be comparatively easy because it follows a set of rigid rules that create a finite (albeit large) number of possible plays. Predicting the intentions of a pedestrian, however, is a more complex and fluid task that is hard to reduce to rules. No doubt that is true, but I think there is a bigger lesson in the AI experience that applies to more urgent problems. Let's call it the vaccine-vaccination paradox.

Anyone familiar with biology is hugely impressed by the agile scientific work that in under a year yielded astonishingly effective vaccines to fight COVID-19. Both the Moderna and the Pfizer-BioNTech vaccines use messenger RNA (mRNA) to deliver instructions to cells to generate the spike protein found on the novel coronavirus, which prompts the body to make the antibodies needed to fight an actual infection. It is a brilliant piece of biotechnological work that bodes well for similar uses of mRNA in the future.

Yet even several months after those vaccines were cleared for use, it is extremely hard to get the American population fully vaccinated. In the U.S., the difficulties have included the vexed politics of the past year, but the logistical challenges turned out to be great as well. Before the vaccines were authorized, some health experts were concerned that there might not be enough vials and syringes or cold storage. Others noted the problem of vaccine hesitancy. And since the vaccines became available, a host of new problems, including such quotidian tasks as scheduling, have plagued the program. The hard task of creating a vaccine proved (relatively) easy; the easy task of vaccination has proved very hard.

Maybe it is time to rethink our categories. We view chess as hard because very few people can play it at a high level, and almost no one is a grand master. In contrast, there are nearly four million nurses in the U.S. alone, most of whom presumably know how to deliver inoculations. If we had to, nearly all of us could probably learn to drive a truck to deliver vaccines. But this perspective confuses difficulty with scarcity. As the AI example shows, many things that all of us can do are in some respects remarkably difficult. Or perhaps we are conflating what is difficult to conceive with what is a challenge to do. Quantum physics is conceptually hard; administering 600 million shots in a large, diverse country with a decentralized health system is a staggeringly difficult practicality.

We call the physical sciences "hard" because they deal with issues that are mostly independent of the vagaries of human nature; they offer laws that (at least in the right circumstances) yield exact answers. But physics and chemistry will never tell us how to design an effective vaccination program or solve the problem of the crossing pedestrian, in part because they do not help us comprehend human behavior. The social sciences rarely yield exact answers. But that does not make them easy.

When it comes to solving real-life problems, it is the supposedly straightforward ones that seem to be tripping us up. The vaccine-vaccination paradox suggests that the truly hard sciences are those that involve human behavior.

About the Author

Naomi Oreskes is a professor of the history of science at Harvard University. She is the author of Why Trust Science? *(Princeton University Press, 2019) and co-author of* Discerning Experts *(University of Chicago, 2019).*

How to Debunk Misinformation About COVID, Vaccines, and Masks

By Kathleen Hall Jamieson

I have spent much of my career studying ways to blunt the effects of disinformation and help the public make sense of the complexities of politics and science. When my colleagues and I probed the relation between the consumption of misinformation and the embrace, or dismissal, of protective behaviors that will ultimately stop the coronavirus's spread, the results were clear: Those who believe false ideas and conspiracy theories about COVID-19 and vaccines are less likely to engage in mask wearing, social distancing, hand washing, and vaccination.

In the midst of a raging pandemic, the importance of science communication is indisputable. Mention "science communication," though, and what comes to mind in this context are public service announcements touting the 3 Ws (Wear a mask, Watch your distance, Wash your hands) or the FAQ pages of the Centers for Disease Control and Prevention. Ask someone what "science communicator" evokes, and responses might include a family physician and experts such as Anthony S. Fauci, director of the National Institute of Allergy and Infectious Diseases, and CNN's Sanjay Gupta, who appear so regularly on our screens that we think of them as friends. But Fauci isn't on your family Zoom call when a cousin mistakenly asserts that the CDC has found that wearing a mask makes you more likely to get COVID-19. Nor is Gupta at the ready when your friend's daughter wonders whether the COVID vaccine contains microchips designed to track us.

It matters how we respond in these moments. As Cailin O'Connor and James Owen Weatherall wrote in this magazine in 2019, the "social transmission of knowledge is at the heart of culture and science." In a large-scale online social network experiment conducted in 2018, Doug Guilbeault and Damon Centola, both then at the

University of Pennsylvania's Annenberg School for Communication, confirmed that power. When smokers and nonsmokers collaboratively evaluated antismoking messages, the smokers were more likely to acknowledge the harms of tobacco use than the smokers who evaluated the messages on their own. Similarly Sally Chan and Dolores Albarracin of the University of Illinois at Urbana-Champaign and I found that the level of Twitter chatter from November 2018 through February 2019 about "vaccine fraud" in the counties of our roughly 3,000 panelists were associated with negative attitudes and lower rates of flu vaccination among them later in the year. But those worrisome effects did not occur among people who reported discussing vaccines with family and friends.

Indeed, a sibling or a friend online or next door is in some ways better able to underscore the importance of behaviors such as masking and physical distancing than public health agencies or experts such as Fauci. It's not only that we trust information from knowledgeable people who are close to us but that those in our lives can find opportune moments to explain why preventive behaviors are important to them and why they trust the science that says those actions reduce the spread of the virus. A neighbor or a friend can respond with messages tailored to a person's interests and concerns. In addition to correcting misconceptions in real time, a confidant can create an environment inhospitable to misinformation in the first place. Finally, and critically, deception and debunking usually occur in different venues: those who are exposed to misconceptions rarely encounter the fact-checks.

Equipped with a few tools, we can each become part of a larger misinformation-fighting system—as I like to call it, a science defense system. To see the power of such a role, consider the limitations of the first line of defense against online deception: the willingness of platforms to block it. Even when this happens, there is a lag between the appearance of harmful content, its detection, and its removal. Take the 26-minute viral video "Plandemic" that appeared online last May. Despite efforts by the major platforms to remove it, within weeks that video managed to reach millions with dangerously false claims (example: certain flu vaccines contain the coronavirus, and wearing a mask activates it). Like a game of Whac-A-Mole, when one platform bans a piece of content, the purveyors of deception simply repost it on another one or share it in invitation-only corners of a platform or in private groups. Last March even as Facebook was clamping down on misinformation and conspiracy theories about COVID, a *Politico* report on thousands of posts found that the supposedly interdicted content was still on the platform, surviving and spreading harm.

Fact-checking organizations such as PolitiFact and FactCheck.org (which I co-founded in 2003) provide a second barrier in the science defense system. Facebook surfaces the work of many of these groups when a user searches for content that has been flagged for containing misinformation. In a 2015 study, Leticia Bode and Emily K. Vraga, both then at the University of Wisconsin–Madison, found that this kind of corrective juxtapositioning can reduce users' misperceptions. Later, in a 2018 study, Bode and Vraga found that corrections offered by someone's contacts on a simulated social media platform also reduced misperceptions. That conclusion led them to recommend that when it comes to emerging health issues, knowledgeable people online should employ material from appropriate health sources to "refute false or misleading health information clearly, simply, and with evidence." A team of medical doctors at CriticaScience is pioneering this form of online engagement. With support from the Robert Wood Johnson Foundation, my FactCheck.org colleagues and I are seeking to develop new ways to arm the public against COVID-related deception.

When misinformation circumvents blocking, fact-checking, and response by online interlocutors—as it too often does—the last line of defense is real-world relationships: family, friends, and office buddies. Enlisting in a science defense system requires a commitment to make health-promoting practices the norm in one's community, a willingness to bookmark and turn to public health and fact-checking sites for knowledge about COVID and vaccination, a few premises about the nature and limits of scientific claims, a set of realistic goals, and a strategy for depoliticizing the science if the situation requires it.

Every layer in the model—blocking on platforms, fact-checking, online engagement, and creation of a science-friendly community—has limitations. Each additional layer of defense, however, slows the advance of deceptions that, to appropriate a truism, will otherwise get halfway around the world before the truth gets its boots on. And in the case of COVID-19, there are at least two areas where the benefits are so great that they are worthy of concentrated attention: masking and vaccination.

1. Find—and Bookmark—the Facts That Matter

We trust experts to provide us with information that we can't gather for ourselves. If you trust that the FDA's list of the ingredients in the Pfizer/BioNTech COVID-19 vaccine is accurate (a list you can find in the FDA's scope of authorization letter on the agency's site), then that trust and knowledge buffer you from the allegation that the shot injects nano-tracking devices into your arm.

A key question, of course, is: How trustworthy do most U.S. adults consider those who certify health science? The answer, from a *New York Times*/Siena College poll conducted last June, contains both bad and good news. Ninety percent of Democrats trust medical experts, but only 75 percent of Republicans do, which means that appeals to experts such as Fauci and entities such as the FDA will have trouble gaining traction with one out of four GOP loyalists. Yet even in these polarized times, a majority of Americans—84 percent of the U.S. population—say they trust medical scientists, and 77 percent say the same about the CDC.

To get started on stocking a science defense tool kit, then, bookmark the CDC's page addressing frequently asked questions about COVID-19. Do the same for reliable fact-checking groups such as the Associated Press, Reuters, *USA Today*, the *Washington Post*, PolitiFact, and FactCheck.org. To assess their usefulness, try this scenario: Imagine a friend says that a CDC study found that masks are ineffective and wonders whether Donald Trump got it right when he told a town hall audience that a study found that "85 percent of the people that wear masks catch" the virus. The first thing the search reveals is that all the major fact-checkers independently arrived at the same answer to your question. From the Associated Press: "Posts misrepresent CDC study examining mask use"; from *USA Today*: "Fact check: CDC report doesn't show mask-wearers are more likely to contract COVID-19"; from Reuters: "Fact check: Misrepresented CDC study about community exposure to the new coronavirus." Want to see whether the fact-checkers got the study right? The Reuters and FactCheck.org articles each contain a link to the original CDC study.

The fact-checkers all agree that in the study in question, those who got COVID-19 and those who didn't were equally likely to report mask wearing. Those who were infected, however, were more likely to have eaten in a restaurant or to say that they had been within six feet of a person infected with COVID-19. Because our meta-analysis of studies focused on debunking misinformation showed that detailed explanations can be effective, these kinds of specifics should increase the persuasive power of a correction. In other words, a corrective should point out that the maskers in that study who became infected were more likely to have engaged in behavior that increased their risk. You can't put food in your mouth while wearing a mask, and in the presence of an infected person, masks provide some but not complete protection.

2. Remember That Science Is Messy and Provisional

Science is an ongoing search for knowledge that yields caveated insights. Yet scientists and reporters sometimes cause confusion by implying that a scientific finding is beyond dispute or by delivering it in a story line that invites that inference. Our analyses, conducted under a grant from the Rita Allen Foundation, revealed that a typical news account casts a new scientific finding as a linear quest by researchers who surmount challenges as they engage in a journey that culminates in "discovery" and, with it, reliable knowledge. Students of literature will recognize this story structure as a classic quest narrative that generally resolves itself with no loose ends.

In news accounts of scientific discovery, the quest story line is pervasive. Our review of more than 600 articles about science published in major news outlets from 2013 to 2018 found that most of the write-ups ignored the false starts, trial and error, and serendipity that characterize the scientific process. Most also failed to note that unanswered questions remained. But as *New York Times* science writer Carl Zimmer notes, a scientific article is "never a revelation of absolute truth. At best it's a status report."

With the iterative, provisional nature of science in mind, the *Washington Post*'s FAQ on masks and COVID-19 declares, "Please keep in mind that as the [novel] coronavirus continues to be studied and understood, masking advice may change, and we will update this FAQ accordingly." Ignoring that insight, some, including Trump, have misinterpreted or misrepresented a statement about masks that Fauci made early last March. "Fauci said, 'Don't wear a mask,' right?" Trump told NBC's Savannah Guthrie at a town hall last October. "Then he changed his mind."

A related selectively edited viral video clip showing Fauci saying people "should not be walking around with masks" has been viewed millions of times on Facebook, YouTube, and Twitter. Attacks based on that out-of-context quotation fail to recognize that scientific knowledge is always subject to updating as new evidence emerges. Between early March and the April 3 CDC recommendation that everyone wear masks when in contact with people outside their bubble, scientists learned that those experiencing no symptoms could transmit the coronavirus. Not until October was that agency confident that airborne spread was occurring. Complicating the messaging was the fact that early in the pandemic, hospitals experiencing a surge in COVID patients had too few masks to protect their doctors and nurses. Until mask production could be ramped up, there was a need to reserve the N95 respirators and surgical masks for health-care workers and first responders. Fauci made that point as well.

In context, what he told Jon LaPook of *60 Minutes* on March 8, 2020, was,

"The masks are important for someone who's infected to prevent them from infecting someone else.... Right now in the United States, people should not be walking around with masks.... [W]hen you think masks, you should think of health-care providers needing them and people who are ill.... I'm not against it [mask wearing]. If you want to do it, that's fine."

LaPook: "But it can lead to a [mask shortage]?"

Fauci: "Exactly, that's the point. It could lead to a shortage of masks for the people who really need it."

So when someone in your social circle says that the director of the National Institute of Allergy and Infectious Diseases should not be trusted because he once said, "people should not be walking around with masks," remind them that, as FactCheck.org has pointed out, when he made that recommendation he was referring to people who weren't infected, and at the time scientists had not yet confirmed that asymptomatic transmission was happening or that the virus was airborne.

Another reason to bookmark the CDC site is that it provides accurate content, context, and caveats. When it comes to facial coverings, the CDC says: "Masks are a simple barrier to help prevent your respiratory droplets from reaching others. Studies show that masks reduce the spray of droplets when worn over the nose and mouth." Note the words "help" and "reduce." If a person knows that when scientists say "masks work" they are saying that masks "help prevent" and "reduce" viral spread, they will be less likely to mistakenly conclude that a mask wearer getting infected means that masks do nothing.

Caveats also matter when it comes to vaccination. Rather than categorically declaring that the Pfizer COVID-19 vaccine is safe, the CDC instead reports that the "data [about the FDA-authorized Pfizer-BioNTech COVID-19 vaccine] demonstrate that the known and potential benefits of this vaccine outweigh the known and potential harms of becoming infected with the coronavirus disease 2019 (COVID19)." A small risk: a few of the multitudes being vaccinated have experienced what the CDC characterizes as a severe allergic reaction–that is, one that is treated with epinephrine or an EpiPen on-site or that requires hospitalization. A major benefit: taking two doses of the Pfizer or Moderna vaccine dramatically reduces the chances that the name of the vaccinated person will be added to the list of half a million Americans whose lives have been cut short by COVID-19.

3. Set Norms by Modeling Good Behavior

For decades before COVID-19 upended our lives, public health officials, school nurses, family physicians, and our parents reminded us that to minimize contagion during cold and flu season, we should frequently wash our hands and stay away from others when coughing or sniffling. Because social norms powerfully shape what we do and because we saw evidence in our lives that these practices reduced transmission of colds and the seasonal flu, we and our families and friends practiced and preached them. As a result of that combination of knowledge and norms, our survey early last March found that even before ubiquitous health messages urged us to do so, almost nine in 10 in the U.S. (87 percent) had responded to word of a new respiratory virus by increasing hand hygiene and keeping a distance from those with respiratory symptoms.

The lesson: By reinforcing and modeling a behavior such as mask wearing, science champions can make it a norm in their social circles. We should also remind ourselves that overwhelming numbers do believe in masking up. A poll that the Kaiser Family Foundation conducted last December found that about three in four U.S. adults report doing so every time they leave home.

4. Depoliticize the Science

As psychological reactance theory predicts, injunctions are more likely to elicit counterargument than acceptance; as the proverb tells us, you catch more flies with honey than with vinegar. An effective science defender will listen to a person's reasons for not masking or vaccinating and share counterevidence without questioning their competence, good will, or intelligence.

"The Battle Between the Masked and the Masked-Nots Unveils Political Rifts," an NPR headline noted last May. Because mask avoidance has for some become a sign of commitment to conservative politics, the artful science advocate will marshal instances in which those of like ideological bent have championed the behavior, as former senate majority leader Mitch McConnell of Kentucky did in 2020 and as former New Jersey governor Chris Christie did in an op-ed in the *Wall Street Journal*, explaining how getting infected with COVID-19 led him to conclude, as the headline said, "I Should Have Worn a Mask." Conversion narratives like Christie's or, on the vaccination front, like that of physician Eugenia South ("I'm a Black doctor who didn't trust the Covid vaccine. Here's what changed my mind") can be powerful. My co-authors and I saw that power in action in our study of how people reacted to environmental activist Mark Lynas's explanation of why he once opposed but now favors genetically modified crops. The people exposed to his conversion account were significantly more likely to change their attitudes about genetically modified crops than those who were presented only with his arguments about their benefits.

5. Consider Before You "Like"

When we click a "like" button on social media, we signal that the content is both acceptable and accepted. By sharing, we invest it with our credibility. Not only do the thumbs-up icon and the retweet symbol serve as signals of community approval, but they also invite our friends to join us in reinforcing the sentiments of our in-group. This process of signaling agreement is agnostic about whether it is used to spread science or viral deception (VD).

In a fashion analogous to that of the original VD, venereal disease, viral deception is contagious and socially transmitted. So, as the editors of *Scientific American* recommended in September 2019, "Before you click 'like,' hit 'pause.'" If the message is VD, quarantine it. If the science comes from a reliable source and is consistent with what you see on the Web sites of the CDC or the National Institutes of Health, give it a boost by clicking "send," "like," and "share."

6. Set Realistic Goals

One of the things that my colleague Joe Cappella and I found in our decade-long study of talk radio was that faithful listeners adopted the arguments and idioms of the hosts who served as their daytime companions. In addition to schooling the members of his audience in ways to support conservatism, the late talk show host Rush Limbaugh reduced their susceptibility to arguments incompatible with that philosophy. His success suggests that a talk show host whose audience is hesitant about protective behaviors or immunization could increase the disposition and capacities of at least some people by using the principles of the science defense system. So, too, could a family member.

Yet no amount of evidence or level of persuasive appeal will sway some people on some topics. For them, information will inevitably be contorted to conform to the demands of group identity. Rather than trying to convince people whose minds are closed, time is better spent focusing on persuading those who are reluctant but not opposed to engaging in preventive behaviors.

That said, people who are undecided about a health behavior may be more receptive to new information than scholars once thought. A study published last year in *Nature* upended the assumption that those who are undecided about vaccination are disengaged. On the contrary, these people searched Facebook for information. The problem is they were more likely to reach antivaccination than provaccination pages.

7. Make It About Protecting Your Neighbors

People engaged in defending science in their communities can convey its messages in concrete, local contexts with clear, immediate impact–protecting neighborhood kids, teachers, relatives in assisted living facilities, friends who work at the local hospital or the town pharmacy. If it's a matter of taking care of the community, even doubters might decide to take preventive measures.

A case in point is Gary Abernathy of Hillsboro, Ohio, who, in a July 2020 *Washington Post* piece entitled "I'm Not So Sure on Masks. But Here's Why I Wear One," reported that he cared "about the peace of mind of my neighbors who hold different attitudes." At the same time, he reported that he knew that "the Centers for Disease Control and Prevention reported that 'fear and anxiety about a new disease ... can be overwhelming and cause strong emotions in adults and children.'" Additionally, he acknowledged the CDC argument that "directives meant to protect people, like social distancing, 'can make people feel isolated and lonely and can increase stress and anxiety.'" That combination of knowledge, understanding, and empathy led him to adopt a community norm despite his doubts about the need. "[T]hat's why," he explained, "whether required or not, and no matter how distant I am from a COVID-19 hot spot, I've been donning a mask when I walk into a busy store where most people are wearing one." Abernathy's decisions to mask up last summer and to articulate a rationale for other doubters to do the same qualify him as part of his community's science defense system. And as Dolores Albarracin and Robert Wyer showed in a 2001 study, doubts aside, engaging in a helpful behavior is likely to increase one's belief in its value.

8. Aim for Community Immunity

Wrapping a science defense shield around the concentric circles in which we live–our homes; our neighborhoods; the places where we come in contact with others from our community, such as the grocery store, our child's school, the dentist's office–is particularly important for encouraging immunization against COVID-19. It is immunity within our community–not at the national or state level–that protects us and our families.

When scientists talk about an immunity threshold–that percentage of the population that needs immunity to prevent spread–they are talking about the level required to protect a community. If a high percentage of people statewide are vaccinated against measles, but that number is low in a specific community within that state, then people living in that place are vulnerable. This was the case in the Somali-American community in Minnesota in 2017, where at the time of a measles outbreak, in one county just 36 percent of Minnesota-born Somali children had been vaccinated against the disease. Instead of thinking of herd immunity, we should dedicate ourselves to achieving immunity within our communities from COVID-19, from measles, from flu–and from viral deception.

By relying on trustworthy sources of scientific information, working from an understanding of how science works, modeling behaviors that prevent the spread of both the coronavirus and viral deception, being realistic about the powers and limits of persuasion, and, where possible, depoliticizing the science, we can play our part in our community's science defense system. Doing so will increase the chances that others in our circles will adopt COVID-fighting behaviors and urge those in their social spheres to do the same.

About the Author

Kathleen Hall Jamieson is director of the Annenberg Public Policy Center of the University of Pennsylvania and co-founder of FactCheck.org.

How Communication Around COVID Fuels a Mistrust of Science

By Joseph V. Sakran and Kavita K. Patel

The highly contagious COVID Omicron variant is shattering new U.S. daily case records. With Omicron carrying a risk of breakthrough infection five times higher than that of the Delta variant, we are witnessing a significant impact on the American workforce in all sectors. The increase in cases among essential workers has sidelined many health care workers, resulted in thousands of holiday flights being canceled, and once again disrupted our supply chain.

In the meantime, the U.S. Centers for Disease Control and Prevention (CDC) is adding to the chaos in the way they changed its isolation recommendations. What originally was 10 days of isolation after initial contact with someone who tested positive for COVID has turned into five days of isolation, and upon reentry into civilization, five more days of wearing a mask. To complicate matters further, the CDC has also introduced an option to test out of isolation if a test is readily available (which in the United States is currently not the case).

These changes, which started as guidance focused on health care personnel before it was suggested to the general public, give reason to suspect the agency was motivated by pressure from the business community rather than consideration of the science. As recently reported, the CEO of Delta Air Lines sent a letter pressing the head of the CDC for such a move in order to preserve the airline's workforce. With such a shift from our top public health agency comes a palpable sense of frustration in the country, and the further eroding of public faith in science, the scientific process, and scientists themselves.

For us as physicians steeped in empirical evidence, to think that our health and the health of our patients potentially could be compromised because of business interests feels like a serious blow, undermining even our confidence in the agency.

But perhaps we all saw this coming.

Throughout the pandemic, we have seen how inconsistent messaging around COVID has fueled doubt around science, giving place to consistently messaged misinformation that has found its way into communities all across America. This has undermined our ability to implement data-driven policymaking.

Even before the pandemic, science has been under attack with debates over whether climate change is real, whether tobacco or vaping causes lung damage, whether guns are associated with gun violence, and whether mental illness is simply a chemical imbalance or more broadly related to a bio-psycho-social model.

We have seen anti-vaccine sentiment prevail after Andrew Wakefield's work linking autism to vaccines was published. Dozens of peer-reviewed studies have found exactly the opposite. Wakefield's paper was retracted, and he's been resoundingly discredited as a scientist, but the damage is done. Prior to COVID-19, we saw measles outbreaks reach their highest numbers since measles was all but eliminated. Why? Pockets of American communities, fearing autism, simply refused vaccination. Children died of a preventable disease.

As the pandemic continues, our public health agencies, starting at the very top, need to be reliable, evidence-driven, and consistent sources of information. But the CDC is not alone. Our top drug regulatory agency, the U.S. Food and Drug Administration (FDA), has shown inconsistency that not only affects the general public, but everyone who is involved in health care delivery.

Take Aduhelm, for instance. Several months prior to the approval of the Alzheimer's disease drug, a group of senior FDA officials agreed that there wasn't enough evidence for approval of the drug. The officials said the agency should require further evidence that the drug worked the way the company said it did prior to re-review or approval. This came as a blow to patients, clinicians, and researchers who were incredibly hopeful for a potential treatment of such a devastating disease that lacks therapeutic options.

Despite the setback, the scientific community agreed that further clinical work should be done. Shortly after the consensus decision by advisory members and senior scientists, the FDA controversially approved the drug with no additional clinical studies and zero acknowledgment of the lack of data behind the approval. After weeks of incredible backlash and the resignation of several key advisory members, then acting FDA commissioner Janet Woodcock made a 180-degree reversal that went from making statements expressing confidence in the agency's decision to then supporting an independent investigation that led to the approval of the drug.

That flip left the medical community dumbfounded over the decision to initially approve Aduhelm, which still defies explanation.

Scientists and health care professionals have long viewed institutions such as the CDC and FDA with respect. However, the mixed messages, and the doubt they have created in our minds signal a much deeper problem that will require innovative solutions.

We are entering the third year of an infectious disease war that has killed over 800,000 Americans. At the same time, many more Americans are dying from firearm injuries, drug overdoses, suicides, and delayed medical care. Health care professionals are physically and emotionally exhausted and have worked through some of the darkest periods of this pandemic–whether it's the lack of protective personal equipment (PPE), the personal sacrifice of their lives, or putting their families and loved ones at risk for contracting the virus.

Meanwhile, people are still not getting vaccinated, government leaders like U.S. Secretary of Defense Lloyd Austin are contracting breakthrough cases of COVID, and the American workforce is being crippled by the exponential uptick in positive cases.

It's clear that we are struggling to smother this fire. Part of our success in doing so rests in our ability to restore trust in our scientific institutions.

The leaders of government agencies and the public sector, including public and for-profit health care and research institutions, should create a rapid response system that evaluates the newest data around COVID and quickly provides feedback to best ensure the most consistent, evidence-based messaging is released to the health care workforce and the general public. Similar to the peer review process, elevating the evaluation of significant policies to a larger peer group is a strategy that may be useful.

It's also important to include frontline healthcare workers in these conversations. They are closest to the struggle and often know what the best solutions are.

As an important group of trusted professionals, public health practitioners and scientific organizations must do a better job at communicating our message, especially during a crisis where the landscape is rapidly changing. All of us are prone to mistakes, and while no one expects any individual or organization to be perfect, setting consistent expectations during a public health crisis is critical. The strategy and approach in how we communicate the message, is just as important as having the right idea.

About the Authors

Joseph V. Sakran is an associate professor of surgery and nursing, and director of emergency general surgery, Johns Hopkins Hospital, and senior fellow, Satcher Health Leadership Institute. He holds M.D., M.P.H., and M.P.A. degrees.

Kavita K. Patel is a primary care physician at Mary's Center in Washington, D.C., and was previously a director of policy in the Obama White House. She holds M.D. and M.S.H.S. degrees.

How the Pandemic Remade Science Journalism

By Tanya Lewis

When I first heard the reports of a "mysterious pneumonia" spreading in Wuhan, China, in January 2020, I thought I would write a story or two about it and move on to the next big medical news development. As a health journalist, disease outbreaks are not a rare occurrence on my beat, and most do not rise to the level of an international emergency. But the story of COVID-19 would turn out to be unlike anything I had covered before or am likely—I hope—to ever cover again.

Reporting on the pandemic was like building a plane while flying it—at warp speed in a hurricane. The underlying science was evolving daily, so there was no expert consensus or body of established research to draw on. And there were plenty of people willing to exploit this information vacuum, creating a secondary epidemic of misinformation.

Early on Chinese authorities suppressed information about the virus, and the Trump administration downplayed its threat to the U.S. Testing blunders and shortages prevented this country from recognizing the number of COVID cases circulating within its borders in the critical early phase when we could have slowed its spread. And for months health authorities said SARS-CoV-2 was spread primarily by symptomatic people through large respiratory droplets from a cough or a sneeze or by contaminated surfaces (remember the now ridiculous-seeming grocery-disinfecting ritual?). That guidance was based on how some other respiratory diseases circulate, but of course we now know this novel coronavirus commonly spreads through aerosols that linger in the air, often exhaled by a person showing no symptoms at all.

At the heart of science journalism is a focus on evidence. But one of the hardest lessons many other journalists and I learned while reporting on COVID is that absence of evidence is not evidence of absence–and that even advice from renowned public health authorities should sometimes be questioned. Take face masks, for example: in the pandemic's first crucial weeks, the Centers for Disease Control and Prevention and the World Health Organization said the public did not need to wear masks (despite the fact that medical workers and many people in Asia use them routinely to protect against respiratory diseases). At the same time, CDC and WHO officials specifically told people not to buy high-quality respirator masks because health-care workers needed them–breeding confusion and mistrust.

At the time, I debated with my editor over whether to recommend that people wear masks, against the guidance of these esteemed health agencies. I resisted doing so, in part out of deference to these authorities and in part because of a lack of published studies that masks–especially nonmedical ones–were protective for the wearer. In retrospect, I should have followed the precautionary principle; in the absence of direct evidence, masks were a reasonable precaution to protect against a respiratory virus. That episode highlighted for me just how challenging it can be when the evidence is shifting in real time and even the experts can't keep up. It wasn't until two years into the pandemic that the CDC and others finally started to emphasize the importance of high-filtration masks, which had been abundantly available in the U.S. for many months.

It didn't take long for bad actors to weaponize the confusion to spread misinformation. Patient zero in this "infodemic" was Donald Trump. The former president routinely downplayed the virus's severity, calling it "no worse than the flu." He blamed China, stoking xenophobia rather than urging people to protect themselves and others. He mocked people who wore masks, politicizing a basic public health measure, while promoting baseless COVID treatments. It wasn't just Trump–Fox News personalities and celebrities such as Joe Rogan and Aaron Rodgers have used their platforms to spread falsehoods about the virus and the vaccines. As a health journalist, my job was no longer purely about explaining the science–I now had to contend with politics and human behavior. Actions as seemingly innocuous as wearing a mask or getting a vaccine to avoid getting a disease had become political statements.

There has perhaps been no more consequential or bitter battleground in the U.S. epidemic than vaccines. The anti-vax movement–a small faction but already a potent force before COVID–took advantage of people's hesitancy about the speed with which the new vaccines were developed to spread lies and misinformation about their effects. COVID anti-vaxxers promoted their dangerous claims under the guise of "freedom," never acknowledging that it comes at the cost of people's lives and the freedom to live without threat of a deadly virus. As science journalists, it was not enough just to report the facts and debunk misinformation–we had to engage with the reasons people believe such falsehoods. We learned to use the latest research on how misinformation spreads to try to expose lies without amplifying them and replace conspiracy theories with truth.

All of this has played out against the backdrop of vast inequities in access to vaccines and health care, both nationwide and globally. One of the biggest lessons of the pandemic for many of us has been that racism, not race, explains why COVID has been even more devastating for people of color.

The arrival of new viral variants further complicated messaging. The mRNA vaccines achieved an effectiveness beyond any expert's wildest dreams. But their protection waned over time, and they have been less effective against the highly contagious Delta and Omicron variants, prompting a return to mask wearing and a hastily implemented booster shot campaign. As I write this, Omicron is spreading rapidly and overwhelming hospitals because it is so transmissible. As journalists, all we can do is try to make sense of the evidence as it develops, hope in hindsight we made the right call, and remind readers it's normal, not bad, to update our knowledge as the virus–and our understanding of it–evolves.

Reporting on COVID has fundamentally changed the way I approach science journalism. I have gained a deeper appreciation for scientific knowledge as a process, not merely an end result. I have seen that it is not enough to simply follow the science–that skepticism of authority is warranted even when that authority comes from respected public health experts. And I have learned that science is always political–despite what many scientists like to think. These lessons have been won at a terrible expense. But failing to heed them could doom us to repeat this tragedy when the next pandemic comes.

About the Author

Tanya Lewis is a senior health and medicine editor at Scientific American. *She co-hosts a biweekly podcast, COVID Quickly, with fellow senior medicine editor Josh Fischman.*

Section 3: COVID-19 and Society

COVID-19 Is Like an X-ray of Society

By Leah T. Rosen

In many ways, coronavirus has functioned like an x-ray. With the flip of a switch, it has stripped us of our skin and revealed our internal state, which was once so deliberately hidden, so to avoid the gaze and judgment of the outside world. We are left exposed, vulnerable, illuminated.

In this state, we are confronted with a new awareness: our world as we choose to perceive it does not necessarily match the truth of how it functions. The racism that so many people believe to have been buried in our history long ago now clearly presents itself in the racial demographic data–or lack thereof–for COVID-19. The classism that has divided our society into the haves and have-nots is now revealed with deadly implications, as access to testing or treatment depends on one's connections and ability to pay, respectively. Numerous other forms of inequality and injustice are becoming apparent, as I will argue throughout this piece–each of which provides further evidence to the point that coronavirus is an x-ray that has quite tragically revealed just how broken our bones are.

When coronavirus first spread through Wuhan, so too did the x-ray's exposure: illuminating a pervasive fear of the other, and the xenophobia that follows; exposing how we speak before we think, and the extent to which we project our own prejudice. According to press reports, on February 2, an Asian American woman in Chinatown was attacked for wearing a face mask; and on March 10, another Asian American woman was attacked for *not* wearing a face mask. It seems you're damned if you do, and you're damned if you don't. Consider these stories without the mention of any face mask: two Asian American women were attacked. Our x-ray confirms what it's like to be a minority in this country. What it's like to be a woman.

This is what coronavirus looked like when it was "theirs" and not "ours." But the virus finally did the inevitable and spread to our soil. And so too did the unforgiving gaze of that which strips skin, tears tissue and loosens ligaments. The resultant x-ray image displayed the ease with which we sacrifice our own, as if we had already collectively decided which lives were worth saving–and which were not.

I read a headline on April 20: "73% of Inmates At An Ohio Prison Test Positive For Coronavirus." Now why is that unsurprising? America's inmates are some of our most vulnerable people, and they are also some of our least protected. Should we not offer our most protection to our most vulnerable? We do so with children–coddling them with safety precautions and protective measures, so they feel a bit more empowered. A little less vulnerable. Now think about situations of mismatch: where an individual's relative vulnerability is not mirrored in her relative level of protection. Do you have individuals in mind? Perhaps entire communities? And how are they faring with the pandemic?

Because the prison population is but one example. A community that is overcrowded–in Ohio, specifically, filling nearly 130 percent of intended capacity–insufficiently protected and hence suffering disproportionately. There have been marginal efforts to alleviate this problem, by freeing some inmates, but the efforts themselves are problematic. For one, the numbers released are small, and often even these have sparked political resistance. And I cannot help but wonder, whom do authorities choose to release and why? Because if the release process in any way reflects the incarceration process, something tells me it may not be fair. If white inmates are more readily released than inmates of color, are we not exacerbating the racial disparities in our criminal justice system? Indeed, at the federal level, an algorithm that the Justice Department is relying on for such decisions has raised fears it will produce racially biased results.

In general, data about race and COVID-19 are insufficient. The Trump administration has announced that it will not disclose the details of how the disease is affecting different racial groups until early May–raising the question of whether this delay is being used to gather the most factual and comprehensive data possible, or if instead the delay is obscuring what we already know to be true: minorities, specifically black persons, in our society have time and time again been disproportionately negatively affected during emergency situations or crises. We need not look beyond 2005, when Hurricane Katrina ravaged the same area of New Orleans that is now facing an astonishing COVID-19 infection rate of 1,637.4 per 100,000 people. But if we did, and we jumped back in time to 1927 Mississippi, we would note that of the victims of the state's Great Flood, 90 percent were black.

Now, we are seeing similar trends, but on a much larger scale. As of April 3, black Americans represented 81 percent of COVID deaths in Milwaukee, despite only making up 26 percent of the population in that area. At that same point in time, 70 percent of Chicago's deaths from COVID-19 were black Americans, who make up only 29 percent of the city's population. Similarly, in Michigan, black persons in early April represented 40 percent of COVID-19 related deaths–more than three times their share of the population.

And black Americans are not the only minority group being disproportionately affected. As of mid-April, COVID-19 infection and hospitalization rates among Latinos in Utah were three times those of the state's white population; and there, as well as in Oregon, New Jersey and Washington–three other states that had released demographic data–the proportion of Latino COVID-19 patients was nearly double that of Latino residents.

Moreover, even the racial and ethnic data that exists are incomplete. There has been at least one instance of a Latino COVID-19 victim's body being incorrectly identified and recorded as "white" when deceased. Such mistakes would have the dual effect of decreasing the number of counted Latino deaths and increasing the number of counted white deaths–thus reducing the perceived ethnic disparity. And Trump's hostility toward undocumented Latino immigrants had already made such individuals more fearful about seeking health care. In consequence, such immigrants may be less likely to get tested for COVID-19, again tainting the demographic data.

The pandemic has made it abundantly clear that the well-connected and well-to-do enjoy a degree of privilege that directly benefits their own COVID-specific health outcomes and those of surrounding people, who are presumably from a comparable socioeconomic background. Celebrities and other social elites have been able to be tested for COVID-19 even if they are asymptomatic, when such options have not been readily available to the average person.

If one of these wealthier individuals were to test positive, they would likely have enough square footage in their house to self-quarantine in a relatively comfortable fashion and not put their family members at risk of infection. Furthermore, if they were to develop severe systems, they would also probably have a health insurance plan that would cover their treatment. Now to contrast this situation with individuals who are less socioeconomically stable; they are more likely to live in crowded homes where self-quarantining may not even be possible, not have an insurance plan to cover the costs of COVID-19 care, or might even depend so much on a regular paycheck that they still need to attend work while sick–thus exposing other persons to the virus.

These issues, however, are not the faults of poorer persons, just as they are not the faults of minority groups, or of the incarcerated. The issues are instead rooted in the structural injustices that gave rise to disparities on the basis of wealth, race, ethnicity and criminal status. Perhaps now more than ever before, we can see those structural injustices–illuminated, exposed, revealed. They are, in fact, difficult to ignore.

This, I argue, is the x-ray effect. The coronavirus has spread across the world like a dark substance–blinding us with fear, arresting us in uncertainty. But once we flip that switch, that is, once we ignite the radiation, we are made aware of what exists beneath the surface: all that our aesthetic world has strategically covered up or ignored. And with that awareness comes the responsibility to attend to the issues that have been previously neglected and the persons who have been historically burdened. The examples I offered above are only a few that have come to light since the beginning of our global pandemic. We are also witnessing prejudice against elderly populations, persons with disabilities, rural communities, homeless persons and other vulnerable groups.

So just as an earthquake is bound to first destroy the structures that are least sound, and a hurricane will swallow anything already struggling to stay afloat, a pandemic disproportionately takes the lives already compromised. They are our society's most vulnerable, and our least protected; not for who they are, but for the meaning and sense of worth that our systems have projected onto them. So, the systems are the problem. And the systems are our bones. The skeletal system of our society, which we expect to support us–not to betray us. But upon closer look, from our pandemic perspective, our bones are broken.

No, shattered.

About the Author

Leah T. Rosen is a student in the Columbia University Master of Science in Narrative Medicine program.

COVID Changed the World of Work Forever

By Christina Maslach and Michael P. Leiter

Hardly anyone has made it through the pandemic with their work life unchanged. Millions of people have lost jobs, been placed on furlough or switched to working from home. Essential workers have continued in place but often with major changes to their workloads, including additional safety procedures and an awareness of infectious disease as a new workplace hazard. According to the Bureau of Labor Statistics, employment dropped by 20.5 million people in the U.S. alone in April 2020. Service providers were hit most intensely: 7.7 million jobs were lost in the leisure and hospitality sector, with 5.5 million of them in food service or drinking establishments.

The shift to remote work led to the complete collapse of the work-home boundary, especially for parents juggling child care and homeschooling with job demands. Poorly timed or endless Zoom meetings interfered with people's ability to get work done and sometimes harmed relationships with colleagues. Essential workers often discovered that their employers' only strategy to bridge the gap created by increased demand was for them to work harder–reinforcements were not on the way. Many employees had to deal with inadequate personal protective equipment while feeling unfairly treated. And it became more difficult for everyone to relax and recover from their ongoing exhaustion as entertainment and fitness facilities closed. Because of these changes, workers experienced more stressful exhaustion, became more negative and cynical about the workplace and felt an erosion of self-confidence–the triple markers of burnout.

At the same time, other people–especially those with comfortable home offices and few parental responsibilities–found benefits in working remotely. Being on their own gave them greater control with fewer distractions. The absence of commuting gave people more time and energy while saving them money. People who had been working in unpleasant or hostile workplaces were now free from disrespectful encounters.

The pandemic has taught many people that the job does not have to be the way it was. This realization may be one reason that many are not going back to their old jobs. At the end of 2021, the service provider and hospitality sectors were facing major challenges in enticing people back to these low-paid, heavy-demand jobs, with many positions remaining empty. At the same time, 4.5 million Americans (3 percent of the workforce) voluntarily quit their jobs in November, reflecting both discontent with their current positions and the desire to find better ones. But solving the burnout problem cannot fall to individual workers. The workplace must change. People burn out because their employers have not successfully managed chronic job stressors. We must place a stronger focus on modifying or redesigning workplace conditions. How can job environments be places that help people thrive rather than wearing them down?

People whose work lives got better over the past two years can generally thank personal resources–a comfortable room of one's own–rather than foresight from their employers. But employers can learn a lot from attending to what helped people be more productive and satisfied during this time. For example, workers were less distracted by pointless meetings and open office settings and were able to focus on meaningful tasks rather than being burdened by busywork. Some companies are trying to entice workers with higher pay or time off. Improving job conditions has even more potential for enduring impact.

Work takes up a lot of people's time, talent and potential–and workers are increasingly demanding that it offer a sustainable and rewarding quality of life in return.

About the Authors

Christina Maslach is a professor of psychology at the University of California, Berkeley, and creator of the Maslach Burnout Inventory, a widely used psychological instrument. She and Leiter co-authored the forthcoming book The Burnout Challenge *(Harvard University Press, 2022).*

Michael P. Leiter is an organizational psychologist and president of Michael Leiter & Associates, a consulting firm in Nova Scotia.

The Pandemic Deepened Fault Lines in American Society

By Aldon Morris

In 2020, as the bodies piled up, it became clear that people of color were dying at far higher rates than white people. They had the jobs that exposed them to infections, the comorbidities that made them more likely to get very sick, and less ability to access quality health care than white Americans. The toll revealed in very stark ways that racial disparities and racism were alive and well in the U.S.

At the same time, police were attacking Black people, and those attacks were being disseminated far and wide via new visual technologies. Just as COVID laid bare the racial disparities, the murder of George Floyd unfolded in front of millions of eyes in a way that made racial oppression undeniable. Not only was the structural racism in American society displayed in all its hideousness, but people were dissecting and debating it across social media in a way that had never been possible before.

For social justice movements to erupt, you need a diagnosis of the problem. No matter how much suffering there is, oppression, inequality, and injustice can be thought of as natural. The Bible says, for example, that the poor will always be among us. Some people see it that way—it is just fate. Or defective genes or culture. A real diagnosis was finally on the table, being discussed not only by a few scholars and activists but by Americans at large.

Understanding the depth of the injustice made people angry, and they came out in the streets in unprecedented numbers. In this manner, the pandemic dovetailed with police oppression and technology to energize the Black Lives Matter (BLM) movement. In addition, the pandemic nearly shut down the economy, giving many more people opportunities to protest. During the Civil Rights Movement (CRM), college students were especially available for sit-ins and other protests on so-called T-days—Tuesdays and Thursdays—

when they had no classes. But at the height of the pandemic, far more people had the time to join the BLM and other protests. And there was another breakthrough: for the first time in American history, people of diverse classes, races, and ethnicities joined a movement against racial oppression.

These protests led to important gains. For the first time, there is serious public deliberation on the disparities in health, schooling, access to universities, and wealth that persist along racial lines. The police are more aware of the possibility of being held accountable. And a debate over reparations for slavery has sprung up–something hitherto unthinkable. More broadly, the intersection of the pandemic, police brutality, and modern technology has spurred a very vibrant progressive movement in the country and the world.

How lasting the gains will be is far from clear. Worryingly, the massive social justice movements energized countermovements that are determined to halt any progressive changes to American society. The political right has gathered new strength, to the extent that it threatens to set us back to an era before the Civil Rights Movement. Among the great achievements of the CRM were the 1964 Civil Rights Act and the 1965 Voting Rights Act. What is under attack now? It is precisely the right to vote. Multiple states now have laws restricting the rights of what they call "minority voters," by which they mean voters of color.

The recent Kyle Rittenhouse case, in which a vigilante who shot white people participating in largely Black protests was completely exonerated, is also alarming. In the 1960s segregationists attacked white participants in the CRM, describing them as race traitors. Rittenhouse's assault has similar overtones. Now white people know that not only can conservatives attack them if they participate in protests, but the courts may also side with the attackers. Going forward, will they be willing to risk their lives for a cause that is not directly theirs? And how can we ignore the insurrection of January 6, 2021, when a predominantly white armed mob sought to annul the outcome of the presidential election?

As I see it, a very serious clash is taking place between progressive and conservative forces, between people who are fighting for equality and people who are fighting to maintain the status quo. It is not clear who will triumph. What is clear is that America is at its highest level of polarization in modern history. I can imagine it must have looked something like this prior to the Civil War. We are at a cusp, and we could fall on either side–into the chasm of fascism or into a more hopeful, democratic world.

About the Author

Aldon Morris is Leon Forrest Professor of Sociology and African American Studies at Northwestern University and a previous president of the American Sociological Association. His landmark books include The Origins of the Civil Rights Movement *(Free Press, 1986) and* The Scholar Denied: W.E.B. Du Bois and the Birth of Modern Sociology *(University of California Press, 2015).*

How COVID, Inequality, and Politics Make a Vicious Syndemic

By Emily Mendenhall and Clarence C. Gravlee

It is folly to respond to COVID by focusing only on the coronavirus that causes it, because the virus alone did not dictate the catastrophic impact. For instance, in the U.S., the illness initially hit urban populations hard. But the virus has traveled to more rural areas over time, and recently the impact has shifted to Southern states. In those areas, people younger than 70 years old have been dying more frequently from COVID than they have elsewhere. These same states have had fewer people getting vaccinated and protected. The mortality trends are strongly tied to the increased burden of cardiovascular and metabolic illnesses in the American South, which existed before the virus hit but have made its impact worse. Poorer access to health care has also been a factor in these sad Southern numbers because many of these same states refused to expand Medicaid under the Affordable Care Act. Even before the pandemic, states that expanded Medicaid showed improved health; those that refused expansion did not. As COVID took hold, states with Medicaid expansions were better able to ramp up testing and tracing and to provide health care coverage to people who were suddenly out of work.

The larger lesson of COVID is that social and biological risk are deeply entangled. Viruses may cause disease in individuals, but pandemics play out in populations. This disease, like previous pandemics, reflects political, economic and social conditions. One way to understand these dynamics is through the concept of syndemics.

The term *syndemic* refers to the *syn*ergies among epi*demics*. The idea involves three claims. First, political-economic forces with historical depth lead to entrenched social, economic and power inequities. Second, those inequities shape the distribution of risks and resources for health, leading to the concentration of disease in specific parts of a population. And third, some overlapping diseases make one another worse because of biological interactions.

COVID is not inherently syndemic. Syndemics are not properties of diseases but rather of systems. Syndemics reminds us that, while we can understand viruses in the lab, the distribution of disease depends on complex, real-world interactions among political-economic structures, ecological contexts and human biology. In other words, context matters. Local histories and power structures influence where conditions cluster, how they interact and why some people suffer more.

In the U.S., conditions were ripe for a syndemic to emerge. A deep history of systemic racism and white supremacy in the country had two immediate consequences. First, race-based residential segregation, the racialized structure of the workforce, and racial inequities in the prison system, among other factors, meant that Black and Indigenous people and other people of color were more likely to be exposed to SARS-CoV-2, the virus that causes COVID. In contrast, the accumulated advantages of whiteness meant that white people were more likely to be in professions that allowed them to work from home, reducing exposure. Second, because of the same political-economic and social inequalities, Black and brown people were already suffering disproportionately from poor health conditions such as hypertension and diabetes. There are biological interactions between these conditions and COVID, such as when chronic inflammation from diabetes is augmented by acute inflammation from SARS-CoV-2, leading to an intense immunological reaction that can damage multiple organs.

Such syndemic interactions are likely one reason worldwide excess deaths in 2020 far outpaced the already shocking number of deaths directly attributed to COVID that year. These conditions made the anemic U.S. federal response to the disease in 2020 even more deadly. By continually downplaying the threat and moving to reopen crowded businesses while infections were still accelerating, the Trump administration allowed the virus to spread along the fault lines of society. Syndemic interactions with preexisting inequities in health and the conditions of life meant that the hardest-hit communities were already suffering from concentrated poverty, substandard housing, less access to health care, disproportionate police surveillance and incarceration, greater exposure to air pollution, less access to healthy food and higher rates of cardiometabolic disease. The pandemic made many of these conditions worse. For instance, there were unequal impacts of the economic fallout throughout 2020, and the current economic recovery continues to leave many Black communities and other communities of color behind. And earlier this year, failures to prioritize equity in vaccine distribution allowed glaring inequities to grow.

It didn't have to be this way. Consider the case of New Zealand. There are many differences between that country and the U.S., but they share a common history of European settler colonialism and enduring social, economic and health inequities among white, Asian, Pacific Islander and Indigenous people. New Zealand had, and has, the background for syndemics. But when COVID brushed its shores, Prime Minister Jacinda Ardern closed down the country. Her "go hard, go early" approach, embodied in the nearly five-week lockdown that she instituted in March 2020, focused on protecting her "team of five million." She also urged New Zealanders to care for one another, to be compassionate. The nation has been largely successful in keeping COVID under control. Drawing on long-standing pandemic preparedness plans, Ardern employed basic public health principles to stop the disease in this smaller, less dense population.

Many other countries responded with strong public health leadership, implementing swift lockdowns and controlling the disease. For example, Rwanda's government shut everything down and tightly controlled the spread of COVID in 2020, in part through established trust within the system and what the country's former minister of health Agnes Binagwaho described as "compassionate leadership" in a 2020 *International Journal of Health Policy and Management* paper. A national lockdown ensued a week after the first case was confirmed, followed by extensive contact tracing and testing. Today Rwanda is fighting a new spike in cases by pushing to vaccinate as many citizens as possible, but accessing enough vaccines is difficult because of global inequities in immunizations.

Inequality takes lives. Demographer Elizabeth Wrigley-Field recently showed that Black people in the U.S. experience pandemic-scale premature mortality *every year*. Like the influenza pandemic a century ago, COVID exacted a staggering toll, instantly reducing life expectancy in the U.S. by more than a year. Yet even the reduced life expectancy of white Americans remains higher than it has ever been for Black Americans, and the reductions in life expectancy for Black and Latino populations are expected to be three to four times greater than for white people.

When a novel coronavirus is introduced into that context of inequality and allowed to spread, it is a recipe for disaster–and not only for the targets of racial oppression but for everyone. Another recent study estimated that, if the U.S. government had paid reparations to descendants of enslaved people–an essential step toward liberty and justice for all–then the overall transmission rate of the virus, regardless of ethnic or racial background, would have been between 31 and 68 percent lower than it was. Everyone would have been better off.

If the pandemic begins to recede, we hope the world will not return to a "normal" that was not working for everyone. COVID will not be the last pandemic threat we face. To reduce the suffering from the next one, we must reduce the suffering people experience now. The larger lesson of syndemics is that a more equal society is also a healthier one.

About the Authors

Emily Mendenhall is a medical anthropologist and professor at the Edmund A. Walsh School of Foreign Service at Georgetown University, and is the author of Unmasked: COVID, Community, and the Case of Okoboji *(Vanderbilt University Press, 2022).*

Clarence C. Gravlee is an associate professor of anthropology at the University of Florida. His recent work challenges false assumptions about race, genes, and COVID. It also outlines how systemic racism drives COVID inequities among racialized groups in the U.S. and examines the persistence of white supremacy in American medicine.

If You Think Preparedness Is Expensive, the Pandemic Puts Things in Perspective

By Claire Pomeroy

The coronavirus pandemic has made the importance of sustained, world-class medical research more obvious than ever. The current pandemic is a powerful wake-up call, harkening back to Mary Lasker's warning: "If you think research is expensive, try disease." Her words resonate powerfully as we observe the tragic loss of life and devastation of the global economy wrought by a "once-in-a-100-year" virus that experts had repeatedly forecasted (e.g., *The Coming Plague*, 1994.)

As clinicians on the front lines care for patients, public health experts implement community interventions, and policy makers move to expedite relief packages, we as a nation should grab the opportunity to learn lessons from this dire challenge. We now have the opportunity to gain insights about medical research that can guide us as we continue the battle against COVID-19 and that can help us prepare for future outbreaks. Here's some of what COVID-19 has taught us already:

Good science is key to finding real answers: The urgency of this pandemic has focused the world's attention on discovering safe and effective vaccines and treatments. Touting unproven therapies brings false hope and can be dangerous. The recent death of a person who "self-medicated" with a chloroquine product he had heard about over the internet is a vivid example. The time-honored scientific protocols for generating data on a drug's safety and efficacy using carefully conducted clinical trials, followed by thoughtful FDA review, are mainstays of "good science" and good clinical practice. They cannot be abandoned.

Funding for medical research must be sustained and predictable: Intermittent funding that is provided only when there is a public health emergency shortchanges our capacity for rapid response as new pathogens emerge. Research must be ongoing before, during, and after a disease outbreak. "Stop-and- start" investigations disrupt research. A number of promising vaccines were in development during the SARS and MERS coronavirus outbreaks–but once infections waned, so did the research funding. Protovaccines that could have been useful in developing a rapid response to this novel virus were literally put on ice at the University of Texas and elsewhere–thus handicapping the current development process by many months. Sustained funding is necessary to support the full range of discovery–from elucidating the biology of the virus to developing drug candidates to creating improved systems of care delivery.

Public health infrastructure is essential: The COVID-19 crisis has highlighted profound shortcomings in our current fragmented approaches to health. Chronic underfunding of public health departments, dismantling of national pandemic preparedness offices, and the lack of surge capacity in hospitals have hampered our nation's ability to respond rapidly and effectively. These are issues that need to be urgently addressed in the short term but are also realities that must be changed long-term. This is an opportunity to consider innovative approaches, including global partnerships with the World Health Organization and others, to detect, respond to, and prevent outbreaks of disease when they emerge anywhere in the world.

Technological advances help: We have tools that were not available to us during previous pandemics. This is good news. Telehealth allows patients to access many aspects of ongoing health care without the risk of going to medical facilities and spreading disease to health care providers. New diagnostic machines are available that have been quickly adapted by industry to identify this virus. Teleconferencing facilitates rapid sharing of information among health professionals and others. As we increase use of these approaches during the pandemic, it will be important to integrate these innovations into routine practice.

Support of the workforce is critical: But technology is not a panacea. We must support the people who create and deliver these breakthroughs. The importance of developing a strong STEM workforce is made abundantly clear by COVID-19. We need to ensure funding for young scientists and reduce administrative overload of established researchers. The current failure to provide adequate PPE (personal protective equipment) to clinicians caring for coronavirus patients leaves health professionals feeling like "sacrificial lambs" and fails to recognize their altruistic service. Partisan infighting that slows support to clinicians and other first responders is unacceptable when the well-being of our workforce is at stake.

Investment in medical research is a public good: The COVID-19 crisis will cause immense human suffering and will continue to do so for some time. As we come together to battle the pandemic, we see clearly that investments in areas that improve human health are invaluable. Medical research provides critical solutions in this battle—we have the capacity and, increasingly, the urgent will to create vaccines, develop drug therapies, improve clinical care systems, and strengthen public health capacity. We must remember that once this particular epidemic is over—and before the next arrives.

I am confident that medical science will provide key answers to the current pandemic. Humans will prevail against the virus. But will we learn from this hardship? Once the crisis abates, will our nation ensure serious investment in essential medical research so as to be able to respond to future biological threats? Will we successfully incorporate best public-health practices on display in other nations? My sincere hope is that Americans will step forward to demand that biomedical science be our priority for the safety and well-being of all.

This was originally published as an opinion piece. The views expressed are those of the author(s) and are not necessarily those of *Scientific American*.

About the Author

Claire Pomeroy, M.D., M.B.A., is an infectious disease physician and researcher and president of the Lasker Foundation, which is dedicated to advancing medical research. During her academic career, her research focused on HIV/AIDS.

People, Not Science, Decide When a Pandemic Is Over

By Tanya Lewis

All pandemics end eventually. But how, exactly, will we know when the COVID-19 pandemic is really "over"? It turns out the answer to that question may lie more in sociology than epidemiology.

As the world passes the second anniversary of the World Health Organization's declaration of the COVID pandemic, things seem to be at a turning point. COVID cases and deaths are seeing sustained declines in much of the world, and a large percentage of people are estimated to have some immunity to SARS-CoV-2, the virus that causes the disease, through infection or vaccination. The Centers for Disease Control and Prevention has released new risk metrics that suggest people in many parts of the U.S. no longer need to wear a mask, and mayors, governors and other officials have been dropping mask and vaccine mandates in a push to get back to normal. Although the COVID-causing virus, SARS-CoV-2, is likely to always circulate at some level, there is a growing belief among some people–though not all–that the pandemic's acute phase may be subsiding.

"I believe that pandemics end partially because humans declare them at an end," says Marion Dorsey, an associate professor of history at the University of New Hampshire, who studies past pandemics, including the devastating 1918 influenza pandemic. Of course, she notes, there is an epidemiological component, characterized by the point at which a disease still circulates but is no longer causing major peaks in severe illness or death. This is sometimes referred to as the transition from a pandemic disease to an endemic one. But for practical purposes, the question of when this transition occurs largely comes down to human behavior.

"Every time people walk into stores without masks or even just walk into stores for pleasure, they're indicating they think the pandemic is winding down, if not over," Dorsey says. Whether or not there is an official declaration of some kind, "I don't think anything really has a meaning until, as a society..., we act as if it is."

Author and historian John M. Barry, who wrote one of the most definitive chronicles of the 1918 pandemic—*The Great Influenza: The Story of the Deadliest Pandemic in History*—has come to a similar conclusion. A pandemic ends "when people stop paying attention to it," he says. The rest of the matter is a combination of the virus's virulence, and the availability of vaccines and therapeutics. "We're almost at that point" with COVID, Barry adds, although vaccines and treatments are still out of reach for many people worldwide. Nevertheless, the public has grown increasingly tired of the restrictions of life under pandemic conditions. "We've clearly wearied," Barry says. But he cautions that there is a danger in moving on too quickly.

The 1918 pandemic—which is estimated to have killed at least 50 million people worldwide, though accurate data are hard to come by—is often described as having three waves. The first came in the spring of 1918, followed by a notoriously deadly second wave that fall and then a third, wintertime wave in early 1919—with cases eventually subsiding by the summer of that year. But Barry says a new variant emerged in 1920 and effectively caused a fourth wave. This wave killed more people in some cities than the second one, even though there was widespread immunity to the virus by then. Although many cities and public institutions imposed restrictions during the second and third waves, virtually none did so during the fourth. By 1921, the flu death toll had returned to prepandemic levels. But moving on too soon was a mistake, Barry says.

Ultimately the 1918 pandemic pathogen (an H1N1 flu virus) evolved to become less virulent: it lost much of its ability to infect cells in the lungs, where it could cause deadly pneumonia. SARS-CoV-2's Omicron variant appears to cause milder disease as well, although it is not clear how much of that is because it has lost some of the earlier variants' ability to infect the lower respiratory tract—or because more people have prior immunity from vaccination or previous infection. But there is no law of nature that says a virus must always evolve to become less virulent. It is entirely possible that a future variant could be as transmissible as Omicron and cause more severe disease. The 1918 virus did cause several bad outbreaks in the years afterward, Barry says, noting that one of them—a particularly severe flu season in 1928—led Congress to expand and reorganize the Hygienic Laboratory to create what is now the National Institutes of Health.

For now, Barry is cautiously optimistic about COVID. "I think it's more likely than not that future variants will not be any worse," he says. "In fact, I think it's more likely that they'll get milder than that they will get more virulent. But we don't know that. It's random event. I think, in the long term, that's where we will end up, but that doesn't mean every iteration of the virus is going to move in the same direction."

The 1918 influenza virus never went away (eventually it morphed into seasonal flu), but most survivors developed some immunity to it and simply decided to move on with their lives. "There's a certain amount [of infection] we can live with," Dorsey says. Another factor that helped the pandemic subside from the public consciousness was that it coincided with the end of World War I. Then president Woodrow Wilson and his government were more focused on recovering from the war, and this consumed much of the media attention at the time. "Especially as influenza started to decrease in virulence," Dorsey says, "it was easier to pay attention to the war." Finally, as the flu gradually became less severe, other diseases such as polio started to draw far more notice.

Although it is impossible to draw a direct parallel with how the 1918 pandemic ended, COVID may be headed in that direction. Obviously the virus has surprised us before, Dorsey points out. Even after the immediate threat recedes, society will likely be dealing with its aftermath for years to come. The many people who lost family members and the legions of health care workers who witnessed unimaginable amounts of death and suffering will be experiencing grief and trauma that will make it impossible for many to move on—even if the rest of the world does. And that does not include a potential tidal wave of long COVID, the full effects of which society has yet to grapple with.

As devastating as the 1918 pandemic was, history seems to have somewhat forgotten its horrors. With COVID, Barry thinks that is unlikely to happen anytime soon. "In 1918 people died of infectious disease all the time, so there was a certain familiarity with the experience," he says. That is no longer the case in modern times. COVID has already caused deep and lasting disruptions to society. "It changed everybody's life for a long time," Barry says, "and that is not going to be forgotten."

About the Author

Tanya Lewis is a senior editor at Scientific American *who covers health and medicine.*

Section 4: Mental Health Crisis

Pandemic Year One Saw a Dramatic Global Rise in Anxiety and Depression

By Gary Stix

COVID has posed a threat to body—and mind—for *all people* on the planet—the essence of the Greek-rooted coupling of *pan* plus *demos* to form the now too-familiar noun.

Yet there has been no incisive examination to date of the pandemic's psychological toll on a global basis. It is difficult to determine increases in cases of depression and anxiety because of a lack of data. No good numbers exist for many countries and even whole continents (Africa and South America).

Despite gaps in the data, a team largely based at the University of Queensland in Australia has made an estimate for 2020. "This study is the first to quantify the prevalence and burden of depressive and anxiety disorders by age, sex, and location globally," the researchers wrote in the *Lancet*.

The numbers themselves are devastating. Cases for depressive and anxiety disorders last year are estimated to have increased by more than a quarter—an unusually large surge.

If the pandemic had not happened, the model used by the researchers estimated there would have been 193 million cases of major depressive disorder worldwide, whereas an estimated 246 million cases actually occurred, a 28 percent increase, or an added 53 million cases. For anxiety disorders the number of cases was anticipated at 298 million, but there may have been an actual 374 million cases—a 26 percent jump, representing an added 76 million cases.

The figures for both depression and anxiety usually remain stable from year to year. Such sharp upturns cannot be counted as routine fluctuations; "This is definitely like a shock to the system from what we are typically used to seeing when it comes to the prevalence of these disorders," says Damian Santomauro, the lead author, from the Queensland Center for Mental Health Research, School of Public Health at University of Queensland.

Women and young people were hit particularly hard. Almost 52 million of the added cases for anxiety during the first COVID year were accounted for among women, contrasted with 24 million for men. Although COVID caused more death and serious illness among older people, it was younger people who faced the greatest burdens of depression and anxiety. The category with the highest burden–the 20- to 24-year age bracket–had an estimated 1,118 added depression cases per 100,000 people, and 1,331 more per 100,000 for anxiety. "We are hoping that these findings encourage more dialogue by policy makers, governments, researchers and people considering resource allocation and planning for mental health responses," says Alize Ferrari, one of the University of Queensland researchers.

The university team succeeded in making an estimate for global levels of depressive and anxiety disorders by compensating for the data that were lacking. They did so by relying on other data put together from 48 studies conducted in Western Europe, parts of North America, Australasia and other regions that actually had mental health figures. They were able to statistically link depression and anxiety data to "COVID-19 impact indicators," infection rates by country and indicators tracking diminished population movements for 204 countries. That statistical relationship between impact indicators and mental health data, analyzed for North America and other regions, could then be used to extrapolate the missing estimates for depressive and anxiety disorders for the many countries that lacked that data. All that was needed to make the calculations was the impact indicators, which exist for almost every nation.

Maxime Taquet, an academic clinical fellow in the department of psychiatry at the University of Oxford, who was not involved with the study, praised the effort as providing the first insight into the global impact of the pandemic on mental health. The study, he says, also points to the urgent need for depression and anxiety statistics from the countries for which estimates could only be made with statistical extrapolations. "We need to be quite cautious when we interpret the findings of this study because in large areas of the world we simply don't have any data," he says. Taquet wrote a commentary for the *Lancet* about the study.

The study will continue until the pandemic ends. The data are being incorporated in the larger Global Burden of Disease study, led by the Institute for Health Metrics and Evaluation (IHME) at the University of Washington. Those numbers will surely be useful. COVID's mental health consequences are sure to linger long after any unofficial declaration that the pandemic has come to a close.

About the Author

Gary Stix is a senior editor at Scientific American.

COVID Is Driving a Children's Mental Health Emergency

By Julia Hotz

When COVID shut down life as usual in the spring of 2020, most physicians in the U.S. focused on the immediate physical dangers from the novel coronavirus. But soon pediatrician Nadine Burke Harris began thinking of COVID's longer-term emotional damage and those who would be especially vulnerable: children. "The pandemic is a massive stressor," explains Burke Harris, who is California's surgeon general. "Then you have kids at home from school, economic hardship, and folks not being able to socialize." These stresses could be particularly toxic for children, she and another state health official wrote to health providers in April 2020. Last week U.S. Surgeon General Vivek Murthy issued a similar warning about children for the entire country.

The toxicity has become all too real after 20 months, driven by not just disarray but death as well. As of this past June, more than 140,000 children lost a close caregiver–such as a parent–to COVID, according to research published in the journal *Pediatrics*. Since 2019 there has been a rise in suicide attempts among people younger than age 18, researchers at the Centers for Disease Control and Prevention found when they examined mental-health-related emergency room visits during the past three years. And a study of pediatric insurance claims filed between January and November 2020, conducted by the nonprofit FAIR Health, found a sharp increase in mental-health-related problems, especially generalized anxiety disorder, major depressive disorder and intentional self-harm. These and other distressing trends recently led the American Academy of Pediatrics and two other health organizations to declare that children's mental health is currently a national emergency.

Burke Harris says those patterns arise from what pediatric health specialists term adverse childhood experiences (ACEs). These events include 10 types of specific traumas that range from direct abuse and neglect to overall household dysfunction. The adverse experiences activate the brain's fight-or-flight system—a normal response to an immediate physical danger such as a bear rushing at you. But "what happens when the bear comes every night?" Burke Harris asks. Because adverse events put children in prolonged and repeated danger, it extends their stress response and creates damage.

When COVID disrupted the routine and resources that school and after-school care ordinarily provide, many children were left to face ongoing hazards at home, including parental issues such as intimate partner violence and substance misuse. Both of these problems significantly rose during the pandemic, according to researchers.

As the pandemic wore on, California, guided by Burke Harris's warnings, took some action to protect its children. This October the state legislature passed the ACEs Equity Act, a first-in-the-nation law requiring insurance that covers preventive care and pediatric services to also cover in-depth screenings for adverse events. And, since January 2020, California's ACES Aware initiative has been educating clinicians about nonmedical interventions available to patients facing adverse events, and the state's Medicaid program has paid eligible providers $29 per screening. Such regular screenings—which involve asking intimate questions in a nonthreatening and supportive manner—are linked to a variety of positive health outcomes. A recent literature review found patients associate these screenings with greater trust in their doctors. And clinicians say the screenings help them identify social factors that influence health, which allows them to offer more effective care.

Lisa Gantz, a pediatrician at the Los Angeles County Department of Health Services, is one of more than 20,000 health providers in California who have received free two-hour online training offered in the state. By teaching her how to screen for and respond to adverse events, Gantz says the training has changed the way she approaches clinical care. She remembers one recent appointment with an underweight four-month-old and his mother. "We had gone through all of the feeding [methods], and I really wasn't able to come up with a reason why this child wasn't growing," Gantz says. But when she talked to the mother gently about possible changes at home, Gantz learned the child's parents had recently separated. And the family faced newfound financial hardship—a circumstance true of nearly half of U.S. households by August 2020, according to a national survey.

"As soon as the mom felt safe, we learned that the husband was deported, finances were tighter, and the mom needed to water down her son's formula to make ends meet," Gantz says. "She was too embarrassed to tell me that before, plus a mom's not going to walk in for a checkup and say, 'By the way, dad's not here anymore.' But the screenings create a space to have these larger conversations about what's going on at home." With that information, Gantz was able to connect the mother and her baby with a social worker and to public services that could help them pay for more formula.

Gantz describes the work of treating adverse experiences as creating a "medical neighborhood"—a cohesive unit that responds to the multifaceted nature of children's mental health with equally multifaceted resources.

Efforts in other states are trying to reduce children's adversity by helping parents tackle their pandemic-related problems. In North Carolina, for example, the Raleigh-based nonprofit SAFEchild offers a Circle of Security Parenting (COSP) program. Small groups of parents in the program meet weekly to reflect on their behavior and improve their relationships with their children. Before teaching parents how to listen, the program first helps them feel heard.

That step is crucial if interventions are going to go beyond "telling people what to do" and actually create lasting change, says Ginger Espino, a COSP facilitator at SAFEchild. She notes that many parents in the groups are victims of adverse events in their own childhood. "It's about breaking that cycle of abuse and empowering parents to have confidence that they can meet any of their child's needs, even if those needs were not met during their own childhoods," Espino explains. By inviting participants to affirm their own strengths, talk about concerns, and construct what security looks and feels like within the safe support group, the program aims to help parents create that same loving, nurturing environment for children at home. "They realize, 'Oh, my child's not trying to drive me crazy. My child has a need, and I need to figure out how to meet that need,'" she says.

A few other states have recently introduced efforts to address the surge of pandemic-provoked adverse events. In May Maryland issued an executive order to create an ACE awareness day and announced a $25-million fund to expand the state's youth development programs to every county. And Wyoming is using California's approach to reimburse health providers for their ACE screenings of eligible Medicaid patients, says Elaine Chhean, who assists the executive director of the National Academy for State Health Policy, which co-published a paper on various ways that states try to prevent or mitigate adverse experiences.

Nationally, there have been a few moves to help deal with adverse events. In May bipartisan congressional representatives from Georgia and Utah introduced a bill to expand ACE research and data collection. And that month the nonprofit ACE Resource Network launched an awareness campaign called Number Story. The program, so named because a clinical questionnaire about adverse events gives a person a score based on the number of such experiences, uses conversations with celebrities such as John Legend and Camila Cabello to educate the public about adverse events and how to recognize when they are going through one or more.

Sarah Marikos, executive director of the ACE Resource Network, says such recognition can help change behavior and motivate people to seek help. "In my grandparents' day, it was the norm to smoke, but now it's not. And that's the same thing we want to do around ACEs," she says.

About the Author

Julia Hotz is a writer and member of the Solutions Journalism Network.

COVID Has Put the World at Risk of Prolonged Grief Disorder

By Katherine Harmon Courage

The deaths of more than 586,000 people in the U.S. from COVID since the spring of 2020 have left many millions grieving. A sizable number of these bereaved individuals will find their anguish lasts an unusually long time, does not diminish and renders their life almost unbearable, mental health specialists say.

People who suffer this intense bereavement are frequently unable to keep their job, leave their home or care for other loved ones. Even those who are able to navigate some of everyday life describe their agonized existence as just waiting to die. Their continued high level of stress can damage the body, increasing inflammation and risks for associated illnesses such as heart disease.

This condition, a psychiatric state called prolonged grief disorder, typically lasts for many months after a loss—one year in the U.S. or six months per international criteria. The condition is much worse than normal grieving, says Katherine Shear, a psychiatrist at the Columbia University School of Social Work and founder of the Center for Complicated Grief. And the isolation surrounding so many pandemic deaths likely makes people more vulnerable to it. "There are so many aspects of the pandemic that are going to be risk factors for people having a hard time adapting to these losses," Shear says.

The number of people with prolonged grief in the near future and beyond could be substantial. A July 2020 study published in the *Proceedings of the National Academy of Sciences USA* estimated that each U.S. COVID death leaves, on average, approximately nine close relatives bereaved. If 5 to 10 percent of the bereaved group develops this disorder—which is the standard rate under normal circumstances—this could put the prevalence of prolonged grief at an additional quarter of a million to half a million cases in the coming year. Other data hint the toll could be much higher. A March

2021 poll from the Associated Press–NORC (AP-NORC) Center for Public Affairs Research found that about 20 percent of people surveyed in the U.S. had lost a relative or close friend to COVID. That means a potential bereaved population of about 65 million, and it could push numbers of new prolonged grief cases into the millions.

Because COVID deaths have disproportionately occurred among low-income communities and people of color, prolonged grief will likely have an outsized effect on those populations, Shear and other therapists say. What is especially worrisome is that these communities, and the U.S. in general, do not have sufficient mental health resources—therapists and facilities—to address a problem of this magnitude. "If we don't find ways to bring attention to the emotional suffering that people are coping with right now, it will turn into more serious problems," says Vickie Mays, a professor of health policy and management at the University of California, Los Angeles, Fielding School of Public Health.

A Wound That Time Will Not Heal

Grief can be terrible. Most people, however, eventually integrate their loss and find a way forward, even as they continue to mourn their loved ones. Mary-Frances O'Connor, a clinical psychologist at the University of Arizona specializing in grief and its physiological impacts, likens this process to healing a broken leg: For the majority of people, rest and a cast will allow it to return to normal. Yet for a subset, a complication will arise—an infection or secondary trauma to the area—that prevents it from healing properly without more intensive intervention. In bereavement, those are the people with prolonged grief.

O'Connor describes one patient she worked with who lost her job because she could not get through standard work conversations without breaking down in tears for months on end. Another patient felt it would be meaningless to have religious celebrations for her children after losing her mother. "These types of complications really do impact daily functioning for people," O'Connor says.

The health implications of the disorder can be serious. It can exacerbate suicidality and substance misuse. It is also linked to systemic damage to the body. O'Connor found that people experiencing grief have higher levels of inflammation, particularly the cytokine interleukin-6, which has been linked to increased risk of cardiovascular disease and greater susceptibility to infections. O'Connor notes that long-term psychological and social distress leads to a harmful "weathering" in the body, a well-established state of prolonged biological stress that predisposes people to greater disease risk and earlier health decline.

There are already signs that the pandemic is creating higher levels of serious grieving disorders, says psychologist Robert Neimeyer, director of the Portland Institute for Loss and Transition in Oregon and an author of several books on grief therapy. He sees "worrisome signals" that there will be a higher incidence of prolonged grief. Research published earlier this year in the journal *Globalization and Health* found signs of prolonged grief in nearly 38 percent of pandemic-bereaved individuals from China. That number is more than triple the typical rate, Neimeyer notes.

Researchers say there are many aspects of the pandemic that are likely to increase the risk of the disorder. One cause may be the circumstances surrounding most COVID deaths. "There's a lot of trauma associated with [a coronavirus] loss," Shear says. Whether these deaths occur in a hospital or at home, people are struggling to breathe, and the patient is usually isolated because of infection concerns. "It's happening kind of randomly and quickly and dramatically, and people are suffering a great deal," she adds. "They're not peaceful deaths by any means. And they're also occurring alone."

The lack of contact with a loved one before or during death can add to the likelihood the bereaved will ruminate on alternative outcomes, preventing them from accepting the reality of the loss. O'Connor says that relatives often wonder, "'What if I had done this? What if the doctor had done that?' There are an infinite number of things that could have happened, and that rumination process seems to get in the way of returning to a meaningful life." Previous research has found that meaningful communication with a loved one before their death reduces the risk of survivors developing persistent issues with grief later on. But this often has not been possible in person, or at all, with those who died from COVID.

Another contributing factor for people who lost loved ones during the pandemic—from COVID or another cause—may be the past year of public health measures that limited gatherings, travel and close interpersonal contact. Although these measures have proved essential for controlling the spread of SARS-CoV-2, and the death and hospitalization numbers would be much higher without them, "grief is complicated by taking away so many of the traditional ways you would grieve," Mays says. A memorial over Zoom is "a far cry from being able to really come together with others and experience the consolation of a human hug," Neimeyer says. The restrictions also reduced people's ability to create new experiences and social connections after a loss, a key step in acclimating, Shear notes. The pandemic has increased the incidence of mood and anxiety disorders and substance misuse, all of which put people at greater risk for prolonged grief disorder.

Other pandemic stresses—from financial problems to health and safety concerns—can make adapting to a loss more difficult because they distract people from processing it, Shear notes. This is likely affecting a disproportionate percentage of people in communities hit hardest by the pandemic. Some have lost more than one loved one, some have lost a job and/or home, and many have been burdened with significant financial strains resulting in food or housing insecurity. "When you have a lot of uncertainty, that makes it more difficult to go through a grieving process," Mays says.

Treatment Costs

There are effective, science-backed treatments for prolonged grief, but they involve months of therapy. Professionals in Europe, for example, treat the disorder with more than two months of group and individual therapy sessions to address patients' behavior and responses. Shear's group at Columbia has developed a 16-week one-on-one treatment protocol, validated through research, that focuses on adapting to loss.

Offering such intensive interventions in historically marginalized communities, with fewer financial and health resources and yet more risk, is challenging, Shear notes. In a small study, her team found its treatment program was equally effective among white and Black Americans. But the number of people of color who may be suffering from prolonged grief will likely be high because of the disproportionate impact of COVID on their communities. The AP-NORC poll about losses found that while about 15 percent of white respondents had lost someone close to them to COVID, that percentage doubled for Black and Latino individuals.

Access to mental health care in the U.S. is lacking, with approximately 30 psychologists and fewer than 16 psychiatrists per 100,000 people. That ratio is even more lopsided in communities that have suffered the most during the pandemic. "It looks even more abysmal," Shear says, and it's another aspect of systemic racism in health care in the U.S. According to Shear, many therapists are not aware of prolonged grief disorder, because mental health professionals in general receive little to no training in treating even typical grief.

There are less intensive approaches that can provide some help, Mays says. For starters, she advocates for a safe return to rituals, community support, and communal commemoration and conversations around pandemic losses. "I'm not big on believing that we need people to be in one-on-one mental health services," she says. O'Connor adds that if we can also better alleviate some of the secondary stressors many people are facing–lack of food, for instance–they will be better equipped to recover from loss. "For a person who has sufficient housing and food security and childcare, now suddenly you have the bandwidth to understand what it means that you lost your mom," she says.

As the U.S. works its way out of the immediate viral threat, Neimeyer emphasizes that the need for solutions to this shadow mental health breakdown is growing. "This pandemic of grief is one for which there is no vaccine," he says.

About the Author

Katherine Harmon Courage is an award-winning freelance journalist, editor, and author based in Colorado.

Inventive Ways of Delivering Mental Health Care Thrive During the Pandemic

By Brandon Staglin and Helen Herrman

Struggles with mental ill-health are the world's leading cause of disability. Beset by the coronavirus pandemic, underresourced mental health systems have strained to keep up. But access to care is limited by three major obstacles: a dearth of professional care providers, embedded stigma surrounding mental health problems and a distrust of institutions.

The scenario is by no means uniformly dire. Both the public and private sectors have demonstrated a willingness to promote change. Innovative programs show promise for improving efficient access to care, whether a community's financial resources are large or small. They combine the latest science with digital delivery of information and services and collaborative efforts among people with mental health challenges, professionals and the community at large.

Digital care options through teletherapy and all manner of new apps have seen explosive growth during the pandemic. Online services reach the most remote regions and circumvent fears of stigma for making the decision to seek treatment. They can effectively extend the capacity of health and social services. But they cannot overcome the scarcity of professional therapists. The dearth of providers who coordinate care means that even app-based teletherapy confronts challenges in reaching people in need.

One solution is to bolster peer and community support to extend the effectiveness and reach of in-person and online mental health care. A major development has seen people with mental illnesses help others by providing peer support to show that they are not alone in their struggles with mental health. People confronting mental health issues assist recovery by building trust among their peers with similar experiences. Care teams made up of peers lead group discussions and serve as coaches for others experiencing mental challenges. Training and support for community health workers also help. Community health workers are lay members of a community tasked with providing basic health care, including prevention, health promotion and rehabilitation services, thereby extending care to more people in need worldwide. Research has begun to show the effectiveness of these approaches even when delivered online.

Public and private sectors in several countries have developed programs combining these approaches. Online mental health support and services such as Togetherall, ReachOut, 7 Cups and UCLA STAND, often co-designed and advised by community peers, have become trusted sources of help and referral for young people, their families and others in distress and coping with mental ill-health. A public-private partnership, Strong 365's NYWell is a digital outreach pilot project to assist young people facing the onset of serious mental illness. NYWell's search engine and social media ads link to a Web site that provides assistance ranging from self-education and online peer support to more intensive professional care. The site has attracted thousands of visitors from the time of its launch in New York State in November 2020. About half of visitors take a self-administered mental health screening test. One in 10 connect online with a peer or therapist, and one in five of those are referred to care in the community. The program is expanding, and a randomized controlled trial has begun to measure its effectiveness. Early findings indicate that youth facing serious mental illness are willing to engage in what is called tiered online care, ranging from peer interactions to sessions with professional therapists.

Continued progress will require collaboration among people with mental illness, community workers, mental health and technology professionals, public and private sector leaders, and others. The programs show promise, however, of furnishing a breakthrough in care for people wherever they are.

About the Authors

Brandon Staglin is president of One Mind. Drawing on his experiences with schizophrenia, his advocacy for mental health science and services has earned many awards, including the VOICE Award from the Substance Abuse and Mental Health Services Administration.

Helen Herrman is professor of psychiatry at Orygen and the Center for Youth Mental Health at the University of Melbourne in Australia and director of the World Health Organization's Collaborating Center for Research and Training in Mental Health in Melbourne. She is an officer of the Order of Australia and past president of the World Psychiatric Association.

COVID Expanded the Boundaries of Personal Space—Maybe for Good

By Gary Stix

The stop distance procedure is simple: A researcher moves toward a study participant. When the approaching person gets too close, the volunteer says, "Stop." The task is straightforward. But it is also quite effective at probing the dimensions of a person's physical comfort zone, or "personal space."

This procedure was integral to a preprint study that was conducted at Massachusetts General Hospital to test changing perceptions of personal safety zones before and during the COVID-19 pandemic. The researchers took advantage of baseline statistics they had gathered from 19 people prior to the pandemic. The team compared them with data collected from a dozen of those subjects after the outbreak began and found personal boundaries had expanded by 50 percent or more by one measure. This marked the broadening of a safety zone—a natural, instinctual one that differs from the six-foot distancing guideline from public-health officials.

The study is small, but it is part of a growing body of social science work trying to gauge long-term mental health effects of the pandemic. Researchers are curious about whether changes to our comfort zone of personal space will persist and whether this zone might vary from place to place. Does its observed size hold in rural Mississippi as well as the Boston area, where the study was conducted?

Scientific American talked with the study's lead researcher Daphne Holt, an associate professor of psychiatry at Harvard Medical School and Massachusetts General Hospital, who has extensive experience in trying to understand how people establish a surrounding space that they can claim as their own. She talked about her recent study as a preliminary step toward new research her group plans to undertake to assess COVID's ongoing psychological impact.

[An edited transcript of the interview follows.]

Q: How did you get involved with this research?

A: I've been interested in personal space for quite a while. My group studies some of the automatic behaviors that represent the building blocks of social interactions, the very basic things that we do instinctually and automatically. One of these instinctual behaviors is the way we define personal space.

I am a psychiatrist. And the illness that I've been studying for most of my career is schizophrenia. And it turns out that people who have schizophrenia sometimes display abnormal personal spacing. They often stand far away from other people. And we've found that this enlargement of personal space in schizophrenia is related to some impairments in social functioning. It sounds circular in a way: you are less interested in being around other people, and so you stand farther away from them.

For everyone, there are tiny variations in personal space depending on how well you know someone. We all have this comfort zone where, if somebody intrudes, we begin to feel uncomfortable. Culture definitely influences personal space. Social hierarchy has an influence, but it turns out that if you control for all those factors—and we can do that in the laboratory—people have a fairly consistent personal space preference. It's surprisingly stable; it doesn't really change over time. We're very interested in understanding the brain mechanisms that govern that behavior. And we've done studies of it using very high-resolution functional magnetic resonance imaging [fMRI].

Q: What have you found?

A: We've discovered that the responses to personal space intrusions show an interesting pattern in terms of how they are physically arranged in the brain. We found that there are "columns" of activation, which are essentially thin stacks of simultaneously activated cortex extending from the middle to the outer surface of the brain, within one part of the parietal cortex. These columns respond to stimuli that are located within, but not beyond, the boundaries of personal space. That's been really exciting because it gives us clues as to how basic sensory information is used to calculate the distance that we prefer to stand from other people.

Q: Have you used other methods?

A: We also use conventional methods, including the stop distance procedure, in which a study staff member approaches a participant in the study until that person says to stop. We're trying to understand the pattern of responses to personal space intrusions–what we call the "shape" of the responses. This is something that is not really fully understood.

We have also used virtual reality [VR]. An avatar will approach the subject, or the subject will approach the avatar in a virtual reality environment. And it turns out that people have a very similar personal space response to an avatar as to a real person. The responses are essentially identical, even though the avatars don't look much like real people. Avatars can look generally similar to real people in the way a three-dimensional animated character can, but they are rudimentary enough so that they can be immediately distinguished from actual humans.

Q: What initially interested you in using virtual reality?

A: The reason we decided to use virtual reality was, in part, because our work could then be easily moved into the [fMRI] scanner. But the main reason is that personal space measurements are affected by the physical characteristics of the people involved with the research. For example, if you're interacting with a taller person, you're going to stand farther away from them. So if you're using real people in these measurements, you're going to have some extra noise in the results that's related to these different physical characteristics. But virtual reality allows you to perfectly control for all these variables and to study their contributions. For example, varying the position or the length of an avatar's arm or engaging in eye contact with an avatar can tell you how those things affect personal space.

Q: You were studying a group of people to understand how they deal with personal space. And then COVID came along, which led you to test whether their notion of personal space had changed.

A: It did seem like an obvious question. We were all suddenly being asked to practice this behavior–social distancing–that's fairly unnatural. We had to stand at least six feet away from other people. A typical personal space size ranges from 60 to 100 centimeters (about two to [3.3] feet), depending on the circumstance.

Social distancing as a public health measure is very deliberate, but the normal way we distance ourselves from another person is mostly unconscious. So the question was: How were the public health norms affecting our instinctual personal space boundaries? With virtual reality, we had this opportunity to actually study questions related to personal space in a virus-free, safe context.

Q: What did you discover?

A: We discovered that personal space was dramatically increased in all the ways that we measured it. We measured it by having a person approach another person or avatar or having an avatar or person approach the study participant.

In all of the measurements we did, we found a significant increase in personal space during the pandemic, compared with the same measurements in the same people collected before the pandemic. We saw this even in response to avatars. So it was clearly not because of an immediate risk or danger of infection.

Q: How much did personal space perimeters increase?

A: Out of a total of 19 participants, 12 people completed all of the assessments, including virtual reality sessions, before and during the pandemic. For those who were assessed both times, there was a 40 to 50 percent increase or more in the size of personal space, compared with before the pandemic, when it was 80 to 90 centimeters [about 2.6 to three feet] for one of the measurements we took. It's now about 125 centimeters [4.1 feet] on average.

Q: So are you going to do larger trials related to personal spacing?

A: We have a National Institutes of Health grant to support a collaboration with some engineers at the University of Massachusetts Amherst who have developed a wearable sensor that can measure distances from other people using sound waves. The way that the sound bounces off of the other objects in the room can tell us whether the person is standing next to a living thing versus an inanimate object. We can actually measure personal space in real time with the sensor.

This study was planned before COVID to measure personal space in people with schizophrenia, but we're talking about using the technology to also study people's recovery from the pandemic and whether some of the persistent effects of it on people's social behaviors can be measured using this method. Ultimately we want to be able to identify the people who need help during this phase of the crisis.

Q: As a psychiatrist, are you worried that these effects could, in fact, be long-lasting?

A: Yes, I think that we're already seeing post-traumatic stress symptoms in some people and that some are more vulnerable than others to the psychological effects of this society-wide trauma. I think it's likely that some people will have more trouble readjusting to whatever the new normal is. We may be able to use objective markers of social behavior, such as measurements of personal space, to identify people who needs additional support.

We've also developed a VR-based intervention, essentially a course or workshop, that is designed to help people recover from the pandemic. It helps build resilience by teaching techniques that may help people to handle stress and challenging experiences or social interactions in their daily lives. But it also targets the changes that have occurred in personal space.

Q: Are we entering a new phase that approximates the much trumpeted "new normal"?

A: We made this very dramatic change during the pandemic in the way that we interact with other people. That raises a fundamental question about the regulation of personal space. Is what has happened during the pandemic going to have an ongoing effect on the way our brain calculates the distance we maintain from other people?

It may be that we never revert back to our previous ways of being in the world. In the case of personal space, it may affect things like how we design office spaces, our homes, restaurants or elevators. Those things may have to change if people are persistently needing a little bit more distance from others.

About the Author

Gary Stix is a senior editor at Scientific American.

Expanding Mental Health Care Is a Medical Necessity

By the Editors of *Scientific American*

It is a classic refrain in psychological research: people are more resilient than they realize. The acute upheaval of the early pandemic era led to a spike in depression and anxiety. A year or so later those numbers appeared, in many studies, to return to prepandemic levels, reflecting the science that says most of us tend to bounce back from traumatic events. But the longer-term disruptions, losses and volatile shifts from hope to fear to languishing are harder to parse. COVID has already killed or disabled millions, deepened economic insecurity and racial inequality, and forced radical adaptations to daily life; its serious effects on mental health and well-being very likely will continue and in ways still unknown.

In 2020 the U.S. Congress responded to the mental health crisis by providing temporary funding for services and forcing the expansion of insurance coverage. These emergency measures must be permanently extended to meet emerging needs—and expanded to tackle long-standing and systemic inadequacies in care. In September the American Psychological Association called on Congress to do just that, along with mandating increases in the number of mental health providers. The *Lancet* COVID-19 Commission Task Force on Mental Health, meanwhile, wrote that the pandemic "offers a critical opportunity to invest in and strengthen mental health care systems to achieve a 'parity of esteem,' meaning that someone who is mentally ill should have equal access to evidence-based treatment as someone who is physically ill."

The idea that mental health is less legitimate than physical health has led to paltry insurance coverage, a scarcity of counseling professionals, and regulatory hurdles that make finding care especially difficult in rural and other underserved locations. Yet research has continued to reveal that the separation between mind and body is a false one: chronic emotional distress can significantly increase the chances of developing serious physical disease.

Talk therapy is especially well-suited to telemedicine, which has grown rapidly as an emergency measure and can be adopted as a true alternative to clinical settings. Video-based sessions work as well as, if not better than, in-person sessions, perhaps because it is easier for people to show up consistently. Insurance companies must continue to cover virtual appointments. Equally important are systemic policy changes to bolster socioeconomic support: it is harder to cope with emotional distress when also worrying about financial security.

Young people, in particular, have been hurt by pandemic disruptions. Many are struggling to see a hopeful future for themselves—a key to resilience. Researchers agree that preempting behavioral problems and mental illness makes more sense than beginning treatment after a crisis. One way to proactively reach more young people is to teach cognitive-behavioral therapy and mindfulness in schools. Using standard textbooks and trainings, students could learn to self-soothe, regulate emotions and form healthy coping mechanisms for stress. Such institutional programs would be especially helpful for the more than two million children worldwide who have lost a caregiver to COVID.

Two other groups of people need dedicated focus: those who were infected with COVID and those who treat them. In a recent global review, more than half of people who tested positive report symptoms of so-called long COVID, including brain fog, lethargy and depression. Approximately one in three survivors has been diagnosed with a generalized anxiety disorder and one in eight with post-traumatic stress disorder. Clinicians must prepare for a surge of patients who need psychiatric treatment. Nurses, doctors and other health-care workers, too, need more institutional support; many still avoid speaking up about psychological distress, fearing (often rightly) that it could jeopardize their jobs. Ending the stigma of seeking care would help acknowledge the traumas of COVID, as well as the burnout that was already endemic in the profession.

The "end" of the pandemic must not signal a return to the status quo, if only because it is not the only global force threatening emotional resilience. Severe wildfire seasons, rapidly intensifying hurricanes and deluges of rain—all consequences of climate change—mean that more and more people are experiencing terrifying disasters and loss. Such upheavals will keep overlapping rather than dissipating. It is long past time to prioritize mental health as essential to overall health. Fostering resilience in a world of accelerating uncertainty depends on it.

The Personality Trait "Intolerance of Uncertainty" Causes Anguish During COVID

By Francine Russo

Anxiety disorders are the most common type of mental disorders in the U.S. But a simple diagnosis of generalized anxiety disorder may not capture the specifics of what bothers some people. A subgroup of anxiety sufferers may experience extreme distress when confronting the inherent uncertainties that turn up in any life circumstance, whether helping a relative with a severe illness or choosing a new route to work that is safe and easy to navigate.

Such people may respond to their feelings by leaving nothing to chance. At work, they appear polished and prepared when giving a presentation because they consider every question that could be posed by colleagues beforehand and memorize possible answers in the days leading up to a meeting. Still, all of the prep work may do little to relieve feelings of painful anxiety.

Psychologists, though, are learning new ways to treat these sufferers, who can be identified through their answers to a psychological measurement known as the intolerance of uncertainty scale (IUS). Patients can then benefit from specialized treatment.

These patients are typical of the ones psychologist Keith Bredemeier sees at the University of Pennsylvania's Center for the Treatment and Study of Anxiety. When encountering patients with a high score on the IUS, Bredemeier may explicitly target enhancing their comfort levels with life's unpredictability as a treatment goal. Since therapy is adapted to patients' salient personality traits, treatment for uncertainty distress may be added to their treatment plans just as treatments for eating disorders, for example, may focus on clients' perfectionism. And therapy for obsessive-compulsive disorder may concentrate on patients' inflated sense of responsibility.

Difficulty dealing with uncertainty was first identified in the early 1990s as a distinguishable personality trait. It is one we all have to some degree, but many of us have it at an elevated level. Like perfectionism or rigidity, it is really a predisposition, not a diagnosable disorder. People who have high levels of perfectionism, for example, are at greater risk of developing anorexia. And someone with a high level of intolerance of uncertainty (IU) may end up developing an anxiety disorder.

To cope, a person may live along a narrow, predictable track. Everything may seem fine to them on the surface, but their risk for developing anxiety, depression or emotional distress is higher—especially if something such as, say, a pandemic wreaks havoc on a carefully planned life.

In the decades since the IUS was developed, researchers have found it useful for understanding why some patients are anxious, devising targeted therapies and assessing a patient's progress. In psychology labs, investigators have probed how uncertainty affects people's brain and behavior. Clinicians have used the concept to develop programs that teach parents of autistic children strategies to help their children better tolerate uncertainty. And tourism specialists have delved into which clients might prefer guided tours instead of unguided ones. Most of all, because the pandemic blew away a sense of predictability in everyday life, the concept has sparked an explosion of research globally to find out how those who typically feel this type of distress are faring in these uncertain times and what might be done to help them.

It Began with a Hunch

In the 1990s Mark Freeston and Michel Dugas were part of a team at Laval University in Quebec looking into generalized anxiety disorder. The focus in the field was on worry. The thinking at the time "was that worry was some form of problem-solving gone wrong or a problem-solving deficit," notes Freeston, who is now at Newcastle University in England. But Freeston and his colleagues saw something different in their patients' behavior. "They knew how to solve problems, but something was getting in the way," he says. The team hypothesized that anxious people might have a negative reaction to uncertainty. Following a "clinical hunch," he says, the group developed the IUS and tested it out.

When filling out this questionnaire, people indicated how they might react to statements such as "Unforeseen events upset me greatly" and "It frustrates me not having all the information I need." The scale accurately assessed subjects' reactions–cognitive, emotional and behavioral–to uncertain situations in which they felt they did not know vital information or could not control the future.

Evolution and Fear of the Unknown

For humans and other animals, fear of uncertainty is a default state, says health psychologist Jos F. Brosschot of Leiden University in the Netherlands. Carry your cat into an unfamiliar empty room, he suggests. No fierce dog or hostile human is there, but there is also no obvious place to hide. Without a safe spot, the animal might be apt to claw at your chest in terror. "In the wild," Brosschot and his colleagues wrote in a 2018 paper, "organisms have survived not by waiting for more evidence of threat but instead by erring on the side of caution.... Those who fled at the first sign of unsafety continued to live and pass their genes."

From birth, humans have to carefully learn the cues that signal safety. For a toddler, safety is wherever their caregiver is. Over time, if we grow up in a secure environment with supportive parents, we learn to feel safe when there is no obvious danger. We become better able to tolerate uncertainty. But for those of us who grew up abused, neglected or otherwise deprived of feeling safe, uncertainty is threatening.

Uncertainty in the Lab

At the University of Reading in England, psychologist Jayne Morriss has subjected volunteers in her laboratory to unpleasant experiences that they may or may not be able to predict, from a mild electric shock to a terrifying scream. Before doing so, she already assessed them with the usual psychological tests, including the IUS. She also ascertained their thresholds for receiving a mild electric shock. Then, as they sat in front of a computer that told them whether, when or if they would receive a shock (or hear a scream), she measured their physiological responses with a magnetic resonance imaging scanner, skin conductance sensors or registers of startle response, depending on the study. Invariably, people high in IU showed greater physiological distress.

One of her studies, published last year and entitled, in part, "I Told You It Was Safe," produced intriguing results. The subjects were told that they would receive a shock at a certain time, at an unknown time, or not at all—or, more emphatically, that they definitely would not get shocked. The surprising result is that those with high IU scores showed the greatest physiological distress during the certain-to-be-safe period.

This seems counterintuitive, yet it is easy to explain. Those of us who grew up with unpredictable danger or inconsistent safety are ever vigilant for harm. "People consistently high in IU have trouble recognizing when they are safe," Freeston says. "Just telling them it's safe isn't enough."

In fact, Morriss has shown in other studies that subjects with high IU need a greater number of exposures to a now safe scenario that was previously unsafe before they have no distress response. In other words, they have more difficulty updating their perception of safety.

Tailoring Therapy

As intolerance of uncertainty has begun to be studied as a separate trait from a tendency to worry, psychologists have identified typical behaviors—often unconstructive ones—that people use to tamp down their distress at not knowing. They overprepare, perhaps memorizing answers to all the possible questions anticipated for an upcoming presentation. Some collect every bit of information they can find online and offline. They constantly seek reassurance from others and look for media sources they can trust. Or they avoid situations with unknown outcomes. If they do not know how they will do on a test, they may avoid looking at their textbooks or procrastinate. They may impulsively make a choice, even a bad one, in order to resolve their uncertainty about something. They may also decide that they know an answer and close their minds to new information.

Bredemeier adapts treatments for these patients at his clinic. To help a client feel more comfortable with uncertainty, he first has them list situations that feel mildly to intensely uncomfortable. Let's say someone dislikes ordering from a new restaurant without first reading reviews or avoids taking a different route to work. The worst situation of all would be delegating an important task at work. The person just cannot do it.

In response, the therapist asks a client to do each task, starting with the easiest one first. A feeling of uncertainty grows, but the person stays aware of thoughts and feelings and reflects on the outcome. Maybe the client wishes they had ordered the usual takeout. Maybe they have found a favorite new restaurant. The outcome is less important than becoming more comfortable with some unpredictability. After a series of these experiments, the client is likely to score lower on IU and eventually reduce inflexible behaviors.

COVID: Uncertainty in Real Time

When the pandemic hit, none of us knew from day to day what would happen. No one knew how infections—or the threat of them—would affect work, school or travel. Nobody liked the unpredictability. Dozens of studies worldwide showed that people high in IU were at greatest risk of emotional problems.

A study published in January 2022 is especially noteworthy. Two years before COVID emerged, a team at the University of Illinois at Chicago used two methods to measure volunteers' uncertainty intolerance during predictable and unpredictable shocks. The researchers administered the IUS self-report questionnaire before the experiment. And during it, they monitored subjects' neural response with functional magnetic resonance imaging.

Two years later, at the height of the pandemic, the researchers asked these same volunteers detailed questions about their emotional reactions to the crisis. Having higher self-reported IU or greater activity in a brain area called the anterior insula during imaging independently predicted an increase in anxiety, depression or emotional distress.

Therapists have begun to target their patients' uncertainty intolerance to help them through the pandemic because COVID's unpredictability exacerbates classic IU behaviors in some people. Some read everything they can find on the Internet, wash their hands incessantly and rarely leave home. Others refuse to alter their routines even if they are putting themselves or others at risk. There are endless permutations of dealing with this continuing state of just not knowing.

As Bredemeier says, "All of us like to feel certain. It's just a question of how much distress it causes us. Intolerance of uncertainty is a matter of degree."

About the Author

Francine Russo is a journalist specializing in psychology and behavior. She is the author of Love After 50: How to Find It, Enjoy It, and Keep It *(Simon and Schuster, 2021).*

Section 5: The Aftermath of the Pandemic

COVID Is Here to Stay

By Christine Crudo Blackburn

COVID-19 will continue in pandemic form, surging in one or more regions and disrupting daily life, until the world reaches herd immunity. With that, most scientists say, the SARS-CoV-2 virus will become endemic—always present but transmitted among people at modest, predictable rates. After several years the infamous 1918 influenza pandemic made that transition, and the virus is still circulating, 104 years later, in mutated strains. Almost all influenza A infections since 1918 have descended from that strain.

As the endemic stage arrives, people of all ages will be eligible for the COVID vaccine, and hospitals and pharmacies will be well supplied with effective treatments for infection. At that point, it might be wise for public health officials to treat COVID as a respiratory disease that is more dangerous than a cold, similar to how we handle influenza and cytomegalovirus (CMV)—by evaluating distribution of a seasonal vaccine, tracking hospitalization rates and educating the public about current risk. We don't yet know if COVID will lead to higher rates of long-term complications than those diseases do, so other precautions may be necessary.

In this future, routine testing might become part of everyday life. People with imperceptible symptoms who test positive would know to wear masks and isolate from others. If we could develop similar tests for influenza and CMV and make them cheaply available to everyone, everywhere, society could end up even safer against infectious respiratory diseases than it was before COVID arrived.

Even if COVID cases declined significantly, it's unlikely the virus would burn out. As long as it was still spreading in animals, it could spill over into humans at another time. Nature is always surprising us. A future, reemergent SARS-CoV-2 could be either less or more transmissible, less or more lethal. The Omicron variant that spread this winter taught us to expect the unexpected. Our world still has much to do to become better prepared for new variants—as well as whatever novel virus emerges next.

About the Author

Christine Crudo Blackburn is an assistant professor of security studies at Sam Houston State University.

How a Virus Exposed the Myth of Rugged Individualism

By Robin G. Nelson

For countless Americans, there was a dull but persistent pain to prepandemic life: high-priced housing, nearly inaccessible health care, underresourced schools, wage stagnation and systemic inequality. It was a familiar ache, a kind of chronic hurt that people learned to live with simply because they had no other choice. Faced with threadbare safety nets and a cultural ethos championing nationalist myths of self-sufficiency, many people did what humans have always done in times of need: they sought emotional comfort and material aid from their family and friends. But when COVID-19 hit, relying on our immediate networks was not sufficient. Americans are gaslit into thinking that they are immeasurably strong, impervious to the challenges people in other countries face. In reality, our social and economic support systems are weak, and many people are made vulnerable by nearly any change in their capacity to earn a living. The fallout from the pandemic is an urgent call to strengthen our aid systems.

Anthropologists have long recognized that exceptionally high degrees of sociality, cooperation and communal care are hallmarks of humankind, traits that separate us from our closest living relatives, the chimpanzees and bonobos. This interdependence has been key to our success as a species. Viewed this way, we humans have an evolutionary mandate to be generous and take care of one another. But unlike early humans, who lived in comparatively small groups, we cannot just rely on our immediate family and friends for support. We must invest in national policies of communal care–policies that facilitate access to resources for people who need help–to a degree that is commensurate with the size and complexity of today's globalized societies.

In a sense, the entanglement of our everyday lives made us all the more vulnerable to an airborne virus that demanded social isolation, blowing up the facade of normalcy in the spring of 2020. The new COVID normal, with its mask wearing, social distancing, lockdowns and closed schools, compelled us to abandon our most basic instincts and turn away from our closest friends and family. It rent the social fabric on which we all rely.

Infectious diseases present an unusual challenge: to combat them effectively, we must render aid appropriately and consistently at scale. This pandemic exposed the fragility and faults in each layer of our lives—from our innermost circle of family and friends to the nation state at the periphery—and the differential risk experienced by any individual's core community. Communities that were already heavily invested in social safety nets with measures such as paid sick leave were able to lower COVID rates. Those invested in the ideology of self-sufficiency and individualism prolonged suffering and loss of life.

New Zealand (Aotearoa in Māori), a country with a long history of reckoning with its colonial past and building community, has been a standout success story in the pandemic. The government there countered COVID with nationwide stay-at-home orders, border controls, hygiene campaigns, accessible testing and contact tracing. The results were dramatic: 18 months into the pandemic, the country had seen only 27 COVID deaths. By late 2021, 90 percent of eligible citizens were fully vaccinated. Although new variants have been challenging these successes, the government remains deeply committed to care.

Similarly, Taiwan defied predictions that it would struggle with COVID infections like its neighbors in China by instituting a 14-day isolation policy for travelers entering the country, stepping up mask production, increasing border controls and deputizing quarantine officers who could help isolated citizens. By March 2021 there had been only 10 COVID deaths in a country of nearly 24 million people. Taiwan has fought each new wave of the pandemic with these tactics. Although we may call on our inner circle most frequently during our times of need, ultimately we must rely on local and national officials on the periphery of our lives to be exquisitely human—as the leaders of New Zealand and Taiwan have been—when they develop and enact health policies.

In the U.S., government support was inconsistent, and citizens struggled to work together to keep the virus at bay. The roots of these problems run deep. Since this country's inception, the dominant ideologies here have encouraged not only individualism but also the dehumanization of certain groups, as evidenced by the enslavement of Black people and the displacement of Indigenous communities from their ancestral lands. This dehumanization continues today in the form of the bootstrap narrative—the myth that anyone can prosper if only they work hard enough—and in efforts to weaken relief programs for people who need help. As a result, even though we now know how the virus spreads and causes disease and we have effective vaccines against it, the death toll from COVID is higher in the U.S. than anywhere else.

There have been some success stories in the U.S.—they can be found in groups that have a fundamentally different ideological relationship to community interdependence. The Navajo Nation, which early on saw some of the highest rates of COVID-related illness and death, ran its own vaccine education campaigns and implemented in-house vaccine-distribution policies. It achieved far higher vaccination rates on its reservations than surrounding areas did. Tribal values that prioritize the group over the individual helped motivate members to get their shots. Unfortunately, in late 2021 the virus surged among the Navajo again, perhaps because of low vaccination rates in neighboring areas.

A microbe revealed the lie of rugged individualism. We are not self-sufficient and independent; we never have been. Our fates are bound together. Taking care of others is taking care of ourselves. With the arrival of the highly infectious Omicron variant, we are paying the price for not having developed strong policies early on and stuck to them. But that does not mean we should just give up the fight. Instead we need to redouble our efforts to provide care and resources to vulnerable community members. The emergence of each new COVID variant is an opportunity to reflect on what worked and what did not with the last one, whether locally or on the other side of the world. Committing ourselves to upholding our evolutionary mandate to help one another—not just the people we see every day but everyone, everywhere—is the only thing that will save us.

About the Author

Robin G. Nelson is a biological anthropologist at Arizona State University. She studies human sociality and health outcomes through the lens of evolutionary theory.

Pandemic-Era Research Will Pay Off for Years

By Britt Glaunsinger

After COVID appeared, a huge number of virologists, biochemists, cell biologists and immunologists shifted their work to the coronavirus, and because of that, the world got what it was desperately hoping for: a vaccine, in record time. Everything worked out better than we could have dreamed—several parallel vaccines, all with high efficacy. We are seeing antiviral treatments roll out, too.

Scientists can leverage all this effort to better understand other viruses and diseases. Never before have we been able to simultaneously test multiple vaccine platforms, head-to-head, in massive global clinical trials. Usually you are lucky if you get one vaccine to trial, and if it fails, you will not really know whether the concept or just the one platform failed.

I anticipate that scientists will use all the COVID research infrastructure to build more vaccines against other pathogens, such as cytomegalovirus and respiratory syncytial virus, and to create mRNA vaccines for flu. Furthermore, most of the coronavirus research has been collaborative. That will stick with people. It will make future work pay off more than if all those individuals went back to just their own niches.

This is not going to be the last spillover pandemic we see. It is not going to be the last public health crisis. I hope that COVID has given the public a sense of how important it is to have sustained investment in science. We don't know what discovery we will stumble on that will be the lifesaver the next time.

About the Author

Britt Glaunsinger is a molecular virologist at the University of California, Berkeley, and the Howard Hughes Medical Institute.

Some Pandemic Health Habits Deserve to Stay

By the Editors of *Scientific American*

When the COVID pandemic finally retreats, the world will be different. We will have lost millions of lives—a tragic disaster that will devastate families and communities for decades to come. Other changes, of a less catastrophic nature, may not be bad things. For example, we will have lost some traditional habits and gained new ones. Take the way we greet one another: In March 2020 handshakes and cheek kisses were abruptly put on the do-not-do list to slow the spread of the virus. Once we're given the all-clear to resume those behaviors, however, we might still be wise not to do so. Even if COVID dwindles to become a mostly seasonal illness like influenza, both potentially deadly afflictions will still be with us. Do we really want to go back to rubbing our germy hands on one another or exchanging virus-laden kisses at close quarters? Not if we're wise.

Greetings are just some of the deep-seated habits that have been cast in a new light by the year of COVID. The virus has taught us that we need a major culture change when it comes to basic public health hygiene. We learned, for example, that mask wearing is incredibly helpful in stopping the spread of all kinds of respiratory illnesses—something people in many Asian countries have known for years. Flu cases have been at record lows this year—the U.S. had at least 24,000 flu deaths during the 2019–2020 season, for instance, but so far about 450 this season. Although it is likely that many factors affected these rates, such as lockdowns, school closures and decreased travel, experts say masking has probably played a significant role. Now that most of us have impressive mask collections and lots of practice wearing them correctly, there is no excuse not to don one in public when you're under the weather. "It's considerate," says Angela Rasmussen, a virologist at the Georgetown Center for Global Health Science and Security. "I really hope that becomes part of our culture and that we are more conscious of how even mild infections can potentially impact other people."

Better yet, if you may be falling sick, stay home. In some cultures, notably in the U.S., going to work with cold or even flu symptoms can seem heroic–a stoic prioritizing of work over personal comfort. This now seems ridiculous. The pandemic has taught us to take community health more seriously and to recognize our personal responsibility to avoid sickening others. All workers who have the option of taking a sick day should do so when they need to, and all workplaces must focus on giving their employees this protection–for everyone's sake. The best move would be a federal law requiring employers to offer paid sick leave. Right now almost 34 million people in the U.S. lack this benefit–that's nearly a quarter of civilian workers, according to the federal Bureau of Labor Statistics. And it is even scarcer among lower-paid workers. Predictably, people who are not paid when they call in sick are 1.5 times more likely to go to work with contagious illnesses, a 2010 study by the National Opinion Research Center at the University of Chicago found.

When companies expand their sick-leave policies, workplaces become healthier. A study carried out during the COVID crisis showed that when one company allowed more paid sick leave and encouraged employees to stay home when ill, more workers self-isolated when they got sick, and the company's offices avoided outbreaks. "This company did everything right, and it didn't have to close down," says Monica Gandhi, an infectious disease expert at the University of California, San Francisco, who co-authored the study. "Going to work when you're sick is all too common–especially among doctors, by the way. We need to encourage a culture to stay home when you don't feel well."

People are also much more likely to send their sick kids to school–triggering outbreaks of diseases that come home from class and infect parents–when they can't take paid time off from their job to care for them. We need employers to extend paid sick leave to include time to take care of ill family members, and we also need government support for backup child care, such as nannies who can come to a home to watch sick children if their parents must be at work.

If we do nothing else, we can at least keep up our improved handwashing habits this year.

The Devastating Loss of Grandparents Among One Million COVID Dead

By Robin Marantz Henig

Think of the dead grandparents and everything they'll miss. All the milestones, the middle school graduations and bar mitzvahs and quinceañeras. All the victories, on soccer fields or piano recital halls. All the ordinary shared moments, dancing to "Baby Beluga," or making banana bread, building extravagant Lego towers, watching *The Wizard of Oz* and cuddling at the flying monkeys part.

And the grandchildren, now bereft and sorrowful–think of everything they'll miss, too. The wide embrace, the rapt attentiveness, the patient rereading of the same *Dory Fantasmagory* book over and over again. What those grandchildren have lost, two years into a ravaging pandemic that disproportionately kills the elderly, is a precious piece of their birthright: the feeling that they are totally and unconditionally adored, "gleaming with satisfaction at being this very child," as poet Galway Kinnell once put it. In Kinnell's poem, it was the parents who made the child feel so cherished, but to my mind, that glow is what grandparents provide best. Not even the most devoted parent has the time to marshal the unmitigated, unfiltered, focused adoration of a doting grandparent.

Scientists have known about the special balm of grandparents for a long time. In the 1980s, the husband-and-wife team of Arthur and Carol Kornhaber looked at 300 grandparent-grandchild pairs in a longitudinal study. Arthur Kornhaber, a child psychiatrist, became interested in the subject after treating a young patient named Billy, who had come to see him because of problems with attention, distractibility and dealing with frustration–symptoms that seemed to ease, Kornhaber learned, when Billy's grandmother was around. As part of therapy, Kornhaber asked the child to draw a picture of his family and describe what was happening. Billy drew a pyramid with himself on the top, running after a football. His parents were beneath him, "happy because I am a good football player." And at the bottom were his grandparents, also watching him play, "happy that I am happy."

That was it in a nutshell: the love Billy felt from his parents was a matter of earning their approval; the love from his grandparents was unconditional.

How many grandparent-sized holes have been created in families like Billy's today, as the United States faces the staggering one-million mark of deaths due to COVID? Based on that figure, a rough back-of-the-envelope calculation brings up an estimate of more than 614,000 lost grandparents because the great majority of those one million dead (74 percent) were age 65 or older, and the great majority of people in that age group (83 percent) have at least one grandchild.

Among that number were, possibly, some whose deaths brought a modicum of relief. Maybe their lives contained more suffering than joy; maybe infirmity or dementia had upended family dynamics. So let's set the staggering toll on the American family at about half a million active, involved, essential grandparents, give or take. Half a million elders who could have looked forward to years of acting as family fulcrum, their presence now abruptly truncated and never to be replaced.

The centrality of grandparents to family flourishing is nothing new. Throughout recorded history, involved grandparents, especially grandmothers, have helped promote the survival of their grandchildren, the stabilization of their communities, and even, according to the anthropological theory known as the grandmother hypothesis, the evolution of the species itself. While the very existence of postmenopausal women has been presented as an evolutionary mystery—Why would a species have evolved to spend up to one third of its typical life span unable to reproduce?—the grandmother hypothesis posits that they served an important adaptive role in our species' early history. Without the distraction of babies of their own, according to this theory, older women in hunter-gatherer societies could focus on the welfare of the youngest generation, providing food and guidance for those children while their daughters were occupied with their next babies. The existence of grandmothers, especially maternal grandmothers, is thought to have helped early humans evolve a longer period of dependency during childhood, which in turn led to the development of a larger brain, a prolonged learning period and a more complex social life. And when having long-lived women in the family helped the youngest generation survive to reproductive age, Grandma was passing along her genes for longevity at the same time, thereby extending human life expectancy overall.

Today's grandparents help out in more modern ways. They support their children's careers by providing high-quality, loving (and generally free) childcare; step in to raise their grandchildren when illness, drug abuse, divorce or a string of bad luck render their adult children unable to cope; and mount political action to make the world better for the youngest generation.

Grandparents' help with childcare has a clear effect on young families: mothers of young children are up to 10 percent more likely to have paying jobs if a mother or mother-in-law lives nearby. Grandparents help out with finances more directly, too; 96 percent of American grandparents, according to AARP, give their adult children some form of financial assistance, most often for help with education (53 percent) or everyday living expenses (37 percent).

Helping out financially is especially common for Black and Latino grandparents, who are more likely, on average, to help with their grandchildren's school expenses than the grandparent population as a whole (68 percent of Black grandparents and 58 percent of Latino grandparents do so). Grandparents of color are also disproportionately more likely to take on the role of full-time caregiver for their grandchildren—24 percent of "grandfamilies," where grandparents are raising their grandchildren, are Black, and 18 percent are Hispanic, even though Black and Hispanic individuals comprise 10 percent and 8 percent, respectively, of the general population of adults older than age 50. Tragically, Black and Hispanic grandparents are also significantly more likely than white grandparents to have died during the pandemic, with death rates from COVID that are roughly twice that of the general population–thereby, in the case of grandfamilies, making orphans of the children left to grieve.

In my own family, I like to think the help my husband and I have given our daughter and son-in-law has made the difference between managing and thriving as they raise their two little girls. COVID undid that benefit for a while. When the pandemic first hit, we–feeling especially vulnerable to COVID by virtue of being in our late 60s–were able to isolate in our privileged white cocoon. But it felt awful not to be able to help our daughter and son-in-law just when they most needed help–as they juggled full-time jobs with full-time daycare for their girls, then aged almost two and almost five. It was agony to be reduced to pixels after having been a regular feature of the girls' lives–including Thursday daycare pickups, regular weekend visits and three or four weeks spent together at the beach every summer.

Then a good friend from high school died after a stroke that might or might not have been related to COVID–this man, the same age as I was, died alone in a Manhattan hospital right down the street from me because his loved ones were kept from visiting–and the possibility of disappearing entirely from our granddaughters' lives became real. Every plan we'd ever made about future get-togethers with the grandkids seemed, on reflection, stupid and audacious. We could die from this.

So our Zooms with the girls, as imperfect as they were, suddenly felt precious–and felt like a way of helping out, in a way, as part of the home-school routine our daughter cobbled together. Every morning at 9 A.M., my husband and I were responsible for remote "circle time." I tried not to notice how awkward it was to have a tea party through those infernal screens. I tried not to think about whether the girls felt abandoned or whether they wondered why we'd stopped showing up. I tried not to notice when the younger one started crying and calling our names as we clicked the "leave meeting" button.

We were lucky; we all got vaccinated as soon as we could, even our older granddaughter, and all the adults got boosted. The little one, now almost four, caught COVID during the Omicron wave, but she got through it with only a slight fever and didn't pass it to the rest of us.

A million people were not so lucky, and their grieving families are still dealing with the enormity of the loss.

About the Author

Robin Marantz Henig, a long-time science journalist, is author of nine books and has written for the New York Times Magazine, National Geographic, *and many others. She writes frequently about grandparenthood for the* Atlantic's *website.*

There Is Nothing Normal About One Million People Dead from COVID

By Steven W. Thrasher, Ph.D.

Sometime in the next few weeks, the official death toll for the two-year COVID pandemic in the U.S. will reach one million. Despite being the wealthiest nation on the planet, the U.S. has continued to have the most COVID infections and deaths per country, by far, and it has the highest per capita death rate of any wealthy nation.

This is an unfathomable number of people dead, yet, mass media are downplaying it. This is despite an empathetic *New York Times* headline in May 2020 of "U.S. Deaths Near 100,000, an Incalculable Loss," and using its entire front page to print names of some of the deceased. As Luppe B. Luppen noted on Twitter, the newspaper's more recent headline was the cruel and callous "900,000 Dead, but Many Americans Move On."

The *Times* is not alone; several large mainstream publications, in complicity with politicians of both major political parties, have been beating a death knell of a drum for getting "back to normal" for months. The effect is the manufactured consent to normalize mass death and suffering–to subtly suggest to Americans that they *want* to move on.

News media are helping to shape public opinion in order for business to return to the very circumstances that have created this ongoing crisis. A return to normal will allow profits to be reaped by people working relatively safely from their homes (the target audience of many news organizations' advertisers) at the expense of people working or studying in person who are more vulnerable.

A few weeks ago, David Leonhardt, the writer of the *Times*' newsletter "The Morning," asked Michael Barbaro, the host of the company's podcast "The Daily": "If [COVID] is starting to look like a regular respiratory virus, is it **rational** [emphasis by the *Times*] to treat it like something completely different—to disrupt all our lives in all these big and consequential ways[?]"

I was dismayed. That rhetorical move is a familiar one to me: Two white men frame what they think is rational, deeming any questioning of their stand as irrational.

Meanwhile, some 140,000 children in the U.S. have lost a caregiver—about one in every 500 children. That is a big and consequential loss, and those children are probably not among the many who are ready to "move on" (another nearly one million Americans can't move on because they're already dead). During this pandemic, Black people have been disproportionately killed by this virus. About 50,000 people have died each month of COVID, meaning several Black children are being orphaned by SARS-CoV-2 *this month*, as you read this.

So *is* it rational? To be calling for the end of life-saving mitigation efforts and saying they harm children when so many have been orphaned here and worldwide?

Is it *rational* for Democrats, Republicans and much of the news media to press on towards what writer Tom Scocca calls a policy of "unlimited" COVID? The Democratically controlled state governments of California, New Jersey, New York and Connecticut all moved to drop indoor mask mandates just days after a near-record 3,958 people died of COVID on a single day, February 4. Even the White House reportedly has "begun hinting at an impending 'new normal,' in a conscious messaging shift meant to get people comfortable with a scenario where the virus remains widespread yet at more manageable levels."

Is it *rational*, when as many people who died of AIDS in its worst *year* (near 50,000 in 1995) are dying every *month* of COVID, to think of the novel coronavirus as a "regular respiratory virus"—and to think that the big and consequential disruptions to worry about are mask wearing and ventilation, and not death and debilitation?

Is it *rational* to ignore the high communal viral load in American society and to not do more to lower it so that fewer people are exposed, become sick, transmit onwards and possibly die?

Is it *rational* for the *Times* to be advertising an event happening in March hosted by Leonhardt called "The New Normal, a Virtual Event on Life and Love After Omicron," which might just coincide with the timing of the millionth American officially dying of COVID?

Well, it depends on what it is you are trying to rationalize.

If you're trying to get people to accept that what the nation is doing right now is okay, and 50,000 deaths per month should be normalized, then it's rational.

If you don't want people to wonder why in just two years, the U.S. death toll for COVID is about 130 percent the size of the death toll of four decades of HIV—while global COVID deaths are less than 20 percent of the world's AIDS deaths—then it's rational.

If you want to manufacture consent for looser pandemic measures in the U.S. rather than more comprehensive ones as the communal viral rate demands, then making these claims is rational.

But it's not ethical to manufacture what I call a viral underclass, and it's incorrect to pretend as though the news media have no role in creating it nor in persuading the public that so many deaths are inevitable.

It's a shame that major news outlets are talking more about moving on and returning to normal, and not running more pieces calling for an increase in government-funded mitigation efforts (more free high-quality masks and tests, upgraded ventilation in worksites and schools) to stem the tide of death. American *norms* (rampant incarceration, eviction, homelessness, lack of health care, poor ventilation and economic inequality) are fairly deadly as is.

Rushing for the "urgency of normal" is "wishful thinking," epidemiologist Gregg Gonsalves wrote in the *Nation*. Intentionally or unintentionally, "the urgency of normal"—a phrase cropping up a lot lately—is evocative of a phrase Martin Luther King, Jr. used in his 1967 speech "Beyond Vietnam" at Riverside Church, where he preached about "the fierce urgency of now":

"We are now faced with the fact that tomorrow is today. We are confronted with the fierce urgency of now. In this unfolding conundrum of life and history there is such a thing as being too late. Procrastination is still the thief of time."

If he were still alive, do you think King would be fighting for the fierce urgency of the very normal that produced all this death?

About the Author

Steven W. Thrasher, Ph.D., is a Scientific American *columnist and professor at Northwestern University in the Medill School of Journalism and the Institute of Sexual and Gender Minority Health and Wellbeing. He is the author of the forthcoming book* The Viral Underclass: The Human Toll When Inequality and Disease Collide *from Celadon Books and Macmillan Publishing.*

How Each of Us Can Prepare for the Next Pandemic

By Athena Aktipis and Keith G. Tidball

The COVID pandemic has killed more than half a million people in the United States and caused the greatest economic crisis since the Great Depression. If this pandemic taught us one thing, it's that we weren't ready for it. The scientific and medical community wasn't ready. The government, the military and industry weren't ready. And most of us at home weren't ready either: scrambling for basic supplies, regretting not having a deeper pantry and struggling with the financial fallout.

But building pandemic resilience is not just a matter of shoring up world disease surveillance systems, improving the governmental response or building hospital infrastructure; it is also a matter of making sure that individuals and households have what they need. That doesn't mean shifting the responsibility from the government to individuals. What it does mean is that governments need to begin a campaign to assist households by giving them information and resources that they need to prepare for the next pandemic–before it happens.

Preparation is something that you do ahead of time. After a disaster hits, you're stuck with whatever preparation you have. If people haven't properly prepared, everybody is scrambling to meet their needs in the moment, leading to shortages and strained supply chains. With proper household preparation, we could have avoided the shortages of essential supplies for citizens and hospitals, because households would have already had basic supplies as part of their pandemic supply kits. Ultimately, prepared households introduce slack in the system that allows all of society to be more resilient to shocks.

We already have a system in place that could–with some additional investment–step in and take up this role. College and university-based Cooperative Extension programs, established early in U.S. history and then formalized as partnerships with the U.S Department of Agriculture in the early 1900s, have a long history of teaching preparedness and survival skills to households. These include basic medical knowledge, food preservation techniques and strategies for building physical and economic security. During the 1800s westward expansion, Americans faced many risks including disease, disaster, physical danger and food insecurity. In response, the government asked agricultural colleges to create networks for educating people about how to survive and thrive in the risk-prone environment of the frontier. Though the frontier no longer exists as a wild, risky domain, the mission of Cooperative Extension continues today, though ever-changing and evolving. Currently the focus of Cooperative Extension is largely on agriculture and farming, but there is a great deal we could gain by restoring the original role of Cooperative Extension in helping households manage risks.

During the 1918 flu pandemic, Cooperative Extension programs in the form of home demonstration clubs helped households deal with the strain. They provided training in home nursing (i.e., how to take care of the sick while protecting oneself) and food preparation/preservation. They also solved logistics problems about the distribution of supplies and food so that people who were most in need wouldn't fall through the cracks. In 1919, a report from the Raleigh North Carolina Extension program explained, "It was through the organized home demonstration clubs that [...] we were able to come through the [1918 flu] with the least amount of loss." Renewing this pandemic readiness and response dimension of Cooperative Extension programs could help us get through a future pandemic with much less loss than we have experienced with COVID-19.

If we had a Cooperative Extension pandemic preparedness program in place before COVID, there would have been a steady campaign that would have educated households in what they needed to have on hand and helped them acquire needed supplies. It could have guided households in building supply kits that included things like masks, hand sanitizer, disinfecting wipes and other basic health care materials. Having these kinds of items in place ahead of time is crucial in decreasing the toll on life, health and the economy of future pandemics.

Cooperative Extension systems could also have helped households put together a properly stocked pantry. Our current norms about what we keep in our pantries (enough food for maybe a week or two) is simply not sufficient for general preparedness–pandemic or otherwise. That doesn't mean we have to go into full-on doomsday prepping mode. One simple thing you can do is keep an extra supply of the dry and canned goods your household consumes most. If you want to take it to the next level, grow your own food, Cooperative Extension programs have a long history of helping households with the skills and know-how to grow that food and preserve it.

Economic stresses have been one of the biggest problems that households have faced during the past year and a half. Extension systems have been teaching basic financial literacy for decades, including how to make a budget, spend effectively, save and not waste. There are many families for whom saving for an emergency is simply not possible because of the daily demands of feeding and caring for household members; this is a broader systemic issue that needs to be addressed. But extension programs can nevertheless help shore up some of the vulnerabilities by providing education and resources to help all households build greater financial security.

Refocusing and investing in the extension system and on household level pandemic preparation could substantially reduce the toll of the next pandemic. It comes at a relatively low cost because the system is already in place. It is also already integrated at many different levels from each county in the U.S. all the way up to the federal government. At a tiny fraction of the cost of our 1.9 trillion dollar COVID-19 stimulus package, we could shore up our collective vulnerabilities by investing in a system that would help households deal with the continued uncertainties of the current pandemic and be more resilient in the face of future pandemics.

About the Authors

Athena Aktipis is an associate professor in the psychology department at Arizona State University and cooperation researcher. Aktipis is author of The Cheating Cell: How Evolution Helps Us Understand and Treat Cancer *(Princeton University Press, 2020) and host of the Zombified podcast.*

Keith G. Tidball is assistant director of Cornell Cooperative Extension at Cornell University and is an extension faculty member of the Department of Natural Resources and Environment. He is an anthropologist who studies cultural responses to war and natural disasters, and has served in the New York Guard in several leadership positions where he deployed for Operation COVID 19. Tidball co-edited Greening in the Red Zone: Disaster, Resilience and Community Greening *(Springer, 2014) and directs the Extension Disaster Education Network.*

Tons of COVID Medical Garbage Threaten Health

By Charles Schmidt

The COVID pandemic is not just a public health crisis. It is also an environmental one. After more than 430 million reported cases of the disease around the world, the pandemic has generated huge amounts of medical garbage in the form of test kits, gloves, masks, syringes and other products that people at clinics and hospitals use once and then toss away.

A recent report by the World Health Organization found the problem was global, but extreme in poorer countries where much of the refuse is simply burned in open pits and decrepit incinerators that lack pollution controls.

According to the WHO's calculations, 87,000 metric tons of personal protective equipment and other medical products were shipped to countries such as the Democratic Republic of the Congo and Bangladesh between March 2020 and November 2021. Most of that material was used and then tossed away. But the WHO's estimate only accounts for shipments delivered by the United Nations and its partner groups, not the enormous amounts of material that countries obtain from other sources, according to Ute Pieper, an independent consulting engineer in Berlin, who advises countries on medical waste management issues.

Medical waste was a big problem before COVID. Many health care facilities were not able to manage waste safely before the disease exploded across the planet, and the vast scale of the pandemic has only made a bad problem much worse. "The pandemic is shining a light on the inadequacy of global health care waste management systems that are long due for an overhaul," says Ruth Stringer, international science and policy coordinator at Health Care Without Harm, an international nongovernmental organization that develops ecological sustainability programs for hospitals and clinics. She served as an adviser for the WHO report.

Ideally most medical waste—related to COVID or otherwise—would be sterilized and then recycled. But for this to happen, the refuse must be split up into its various components, which is a capability that many countries do not have. "One of the biggest problems we face is that the waste is not segregated at the hospital ward," says Amos Gborie, director of the Division of Environmental and Occupational Health at the National Public Health Institute of Liberia. "So, proper management becomes an issue."

Bundled waste in Liberia often winds up in small, poorly controlled incinerators that fail to meet international standards, a common situation throughout the developing world. Incinerator emissions are high in toxic pollutants, and the ash itself is also hazardous. Chemicals such as dioxins and furans, which are classified as "likely human carcinogens" by the U.S. Environmental Protection Agency, permeate the plumes. Their levels can be "hundreds of times greater than what is recommended for atmospheric emissions," Stringer says. "And levels of dioxins and furans, up to 13 times higher than European Union limits, have also been documented in chicken eggs close to medical waste incinerators." Hens and their eggs will absorb these fat-soluble toxins and concentrate the chemicals in elevated amounts, making eggs hazardous for the people who eat them.

Some countries are now experimenting with ways to segregate medical waste for recycling and safer disposal. Hospitals in Liberia, for instance, have recently begun deploying color-coded disposal bins in an effort to sort the waste. Health Care Without Harm promotes needle-cutting devices that prevent "stick injuries" from syringes. "Without the needle, all vaccination waste, including the vials and packaging, is completely recyclable," Stringer says. "We can make that waste disappear." Autoclaves that sterilize medical waste with steam provide further recycling opportunities, and manufacturers can design products with recycling in mind. Masks, for instance, have metal nose clips, polypropylene filters and elastic headbands. Integrated in a single product, these components are not recyclable. But if they can be pulled apart, the pieces can be reused in many ways.

Another important goal, Pieper adds, is to move away from overuse of some protective equipment, especially gloves, which account for a huge share of medical waste worldwide. Health care workers in minimal risk settings, such as people who administer vaccines, often use gloves out of habit or fear of infection, even though "most evidence indicates that the main route of transmission is through exhaled respiratory particles and not fomites [contaminated surfaces]," Pieper says. According to WHO guidelines, gloves may only be necessary when caring for patients sick with COVID.

Beyond minimizing material use and promoting recycling, major environmental benefits "would come from getting rid of the small-scale incinerators," Pieper says. These devices, situated at small hospitals or clinics, are often made of bricks and other local materials and provide cheap options for waste disposal. But they also break down frequently and spew toxic chemicals into the air. Pieper says putting waste in these incinerators can be "no different than open burning." To get past this problem, Gborie says his department recently assembled a team that collects waste from health care facilities in Monrovia, Liberia, and then delivers it to a centralized disposal facility. Liberian officials are also starting to collect fees from private hospitals "to pay for managing the waste they generate," Gborie says.

Stringer welcomes such changes. "Now is the time to focus on creating safe, climate-smart and environmentally sustainable systems," she says. "We have technical solutions, and what is needed is the resource and political will to put them in place."

About the Author

Charles Schmidt is a freelance journalist based in Portland, Maine, covering health and the environment. He has written for Scientific American *about therapeutic viruses that can infect harmful bacteria and about dangerous contaminants in drinking water.*

Contagions Worse Than COVID Will Prevail If Neglect of Global Public Health Continues

By the Editors of *Scientific American*

After Omicron comes pi in the Greek alphabet. And then *rho*, *sigma*, *tau*.... Before SARS-CoV-2 finishes its grand tour through the Greek alphabet, the global public health establishment should do what it should have done long before this coronavirus emerged. It must put in place the basic health systems needed to detect new outbreaks and deploy technologies that allow for vaccines and medicines to be manufactured and administered in low- and middle-income countries.

Because they have often refused to treat COVID as a common threat that demands a unified response, policy makers have yet to thwart the predations of a virus that, to channel the Greeks again, affects all (*pan*) people (*demos*). This myopia means that these mistakes could be repeated when a new pandemic arrives.

The next time could be worse. The National Academy of Medicine predicted in November 2021 that a flu epidemic akin to the one in 1918 and 1919 could prove more catastrophic than COVID-19. The preconditions for such a disaster are in place. A warming planet, megacities, mass migration, intercontinental travel and habitat loss are among the reasons that infectious diseases, like intensifying typhoons and hurricanes, have become part of our lives.

Fast-tracked development of diagnostics, vaccines, monoclonal antibodies and antiviral drugs marks an undisputed medical triumph of the COVID era. Also notable, however, is the failure of governments and international organizations to use our current predicament to rectify glaring public health deficiencies.

The Global Health Security Index for 2021 rated the world's 195 countries as "dangerously unprepared" to deal with future epidemic and pandemic threats. The average score for individual countries came in at 38.9 out of 100, about the same as the 2019 rating–before the pandemic began. Many countries failed to grasp that the pandemic presented an unparalleled opportunity to lay the groundwork for coping with not only this public health crisis but also future ones.

Readiness for a COVID-30 or a new pandemic flu strain–or, for that matter, an out-of-control bioweapon–will require new generations of surveillance tools, diagnostics and drugs, as well as, say, a "universal" coronavirus vaccine that can counter any strain. Having sufficient available vaccine formulations with long shelf lives would also help alleviate the inequities that have accompanied distribution of shots. Underscoring the absence of "global" in "global public health," Portugal had fully vaccinated 89 percent of its population by mid-January but Mali only 2.8 percent.

The most pressing priority should be a return to basics, both globally and locally. COVID has served as a painful demonstration that public health is as essential to national security as a standing army. And the cost of health security is minimal. In 2016 the Commission on a Global Health Risk Framework for the Future estimated that for 65 cents a year for every person on the planet, we could upgrade national pandemic preparedness programs worldwide. An investment of $4.5 billion–far less than the price of a single new ballistic missile submarine–might prevent the global loss of millions of lives and an economic hit in the trillions of dollars.

The basics entail not only building new systems to prepare for pandemics but a major strengthening of institutions already in place. Public health legal expert Lawrence O. Gostin notes in this issue that the World Health Organization has a 2022–2023 budget of $6.12 billion, which is less than those of some major U.S. teaching hospitals. The WHO needs not just money but reforms that give it the authority to better monitor and intervene when new infectious diseases emerge. At the country level, the most basic of basics consist of functioning national systems that furnish medical care for all and financial help, as needed, for child care, food and housing and other measures to waylay the poverty-related chronic diseases capable of sending even a relatively young adult onto a ventilator during a future pandemic.

After repeated outbreaks of horrific diseases such as SARS, Ebola and Zika, perhaps this calamity will prove traumatic enough to allow for a coherent remake of the current system. Deaths from COVID worldwide by mid-January about equaled the population of Norway—and the pandemic is still with us. Only when global public health commands the attention of policy makers in the same way as a new contract for nuclear submarines will Greek letters return to their more familiar role in American life as naming conventions for student groups on college campuses.

GLOSSARY

asymptomatic To have a condition without showing symptoms.

biotechnology Using living organisms to produce useful products.

classism Prejudice against a particular class or preference for one's own class.

depoliticize To remove from the sphere of politics.

epidemiology The study of the causes, distribution, and control of health-related states, such as diseases, in a population.

exacerbate To make a thing, such as a situation or problem, worse.

furlough An unpaid leave or absence from work.

genome sequence The genetic makeup of an organism or cell.

health inequity The unequal distribution of resources related to health.

ideological Having to do with a system of political or religious ideas.

inoculation The artificial immunization of a person using a vaccine of a biological organism to prevent disease.

intranasal Occurring in or given through the nose.

iterative Having to do with the repetition of an action or procedure.

malevolent Showing spite or hatred; acting out of ill will.

nationalism Identifying with, preferring, and supporting one's own nation over other nations.

populism A political view that values the opinions and preferences of common people over those of elites.

provisional Temporary; useful for the moment, but likely to be changed later.

reverse engineering To examine or take apart a product to understand how it was made.

syndemic Describes multiple epidemics that occur at the same time and interact with each other.

veracity The quality of being accurate, factual, or truthful.

virulent Describes a thing, such as a disease, that is severe, hostile, or destructive.

FURTHER INFORMATION

DelViscio, Jeffery. "COVID Dominated Their Science Lives: Here's What Four Experts Learned over Two Years." *Scientific American*, February 16, 2022, https://www.scientificamerican.com/video/covid-dominated-their-science-lives-heres-what-four-experts-learned-over-two-years/.

Knight, Victoria. "COVID Still Threatens Millions of Immunocompromised People." *Scientific American*, February 24, 2022, https://www.scientificamerican.com/article/covid-still-threatens-millions-of-immunocompromised-people/.

Maxman, Amy. "New Studies Support Wuhan Market as Pandemic's Origin Point." *Scientific American*, February 28, 2022, https://www.scientificamerican.com/article/new-studies-support-wuhan-market-as-pandemics-origin-point/.

Miller, Lisa. "What Is a Vaccinated Person's Risk of Dying from COVID?" *Scientific American*, February 26, 2022, https://www.scientificamerican.com/article/what-is-a-vaccinated-persons-risk-of-dying-from-covid/.

Montañez, Amanda, et al. "COVID's Uneven Toll Captured in Data." *Scientific American*, March 1, 2022, https://www.scientificamerican.com/article/covids-uneven-toll-captured-in-data/.

UNICEF. "COVID 19 and Children." https://data.unicef.org/covid-19-and-children/?utm_source.

World Health Organization. "Coronavirus Disease (COVID-19) Pandemic." https://www.who.int/emergencies/diseases/novel-coronavirus-2019.

World Health Organization. "COVID-19 Pandemic Triggers 25% Increase in Prevalence of Anxiety and Depression Worldwide." March 2, 2022, https://www.who.int/news/item/02-03-2022-covid-19-pandemic-triggers-25-increase-in-prevalence-of-anxiety-and-depression-worldwide.

CITATIONS

1.1 A High-Speed Scientific Hive Mind Emerged from the COVID Pandemic by Joseph Bak-Coleman and Carl T. Bergstrom (March 1, 2022); 1.2 The Pandemic Set Off a Boom in Diagnostics by Roxanne Khamsi (March 1, 2022); 1.3 Mobile Clinics Can Help Reduce Health Inequity by David E. Velasquez, LaShyra "Lash" Nolen, and Alister Martin (June 30, 2021); 1.4 COVID Revealed the Fragility of American Public Health by Wendy E. Parmet (March 2022); 1.5 How COVID Changed Science by William A. Haseltine (May 25, 2021); 2.1 The Lab-Leak Theory of COVID's Origin Is Not Totally Irrational by Naomi Oreskes (September 1, 2021); 2.2 A Grassroots Effort to Fight Misinformation During the Pandemic by Lindsay Milliken, Michael A. Fisher, and Ali Nouri (September 18, 2020); 2.3 To Understand How Science Denial Works, Look to History by Naomi Oreskes (December 1, 2020); 2.4 Making Vaccines Is Straightforward; Getting People to Take Them Isn't by Naomi Oreskes (May 1, 2021); 2.5 How to Debunk Misinformation About COVID, Vaccines, and Masks by Kathleen Hall Jamieson (April 1, 2021); 2.6 How Communication Around COVID Fuels a Mistrust of Science by Joseph V. Sakran and Kavita K. Patel (January 6, 2022); 2.7 How the Pandemic Remade Science Journalism by Tanya Lewis (March 1, 2022); 3.1 COVID-19 Is like an X-ray of Society by Leah T. Rosen (May 14, 2020); 3.2 COVID Changed the World of Work Forever by Christina Maslach and Michael P. Leiter (March 1, 2022); 3.3 The Pandemic Deepened Fault Lines in American Society by Aldon Morris (March 1, 2022); 3.4 How COVID, Inequality, and Politics Make a Vicious Syndemic by Emily Mendenhall and Clarence C. Gravlee (August 26, 2021); 3.5 If You Think Preparedness Is Expensive, the Pandemic Puts Things in Perspective by Claire Pomeroy (April 30, 2020); 3.6 People, Not Science, Decide When a Pandemic Is Over by Tanya Lewis (March 14, 2022); 4.1 Pandemic Year One Saw a Dramatic Global Rise in Anxiety and Depression by Gary Stix (October 8, 2021); 4.2 COVID Is Driving a Children's Mental Health Emergency by Julia Hotz (December 13, 2021); 4.3 COVID Has Put the World at Risk of Prolonged Grief Disorder by Katherine Harmon Courage (May 19, 2021); 4.4 Inventive Ways of Delivering Mental Health Care Thrive During the Pandemic by Brandon Staglin and Helen Herrman (September 14, 2021); 4.5 COVID Expanded the Boundaries of Personal Space—Maybe for Good by Gary Stix (October 27, 2021); 4.6 Expanding Mental Health Care Is a Medical Necessity by the Editors of *Scientific American* (December 1, 2021); 4.7 The Personality Trait "Intolerance of Uncertainty" Causes Anguish During COVID by Francine Russo (February 14, 2022); 5.1 COVID Is Here to Stay by Christine Crudo Blackburn (March 1, 2022); 5.2 How a Virus Exposed the Myth of Rugged Individualism by Robin G. Nelson (March 1, 2022); 5.3 Pandemic-Era Research Will Pay Off for Years by Britt Glaunsinger (March 1, 2022); 5.4 Some Pandemic Health Habits Deserve to Stay by the Editors of *Scientific American* (June 1, 2021); 5.5 The Devastating Loss of Grandparents Among One Million COVID Dead by Robin Marantz Henig (March 4, 2022); 5.6 There Is Nothing Normal About One Million People Dead from COVID by Steven W. Thrasher, Ph.D. (February 10, 2022); 5.7 How Each of Us Can Prepare for the Next Pandemic by Athena Aktipis and Keith G. Tidball (May 11, 2021); 5.8 Tons of COVID Medical Garbage Threaten Health by Charles Schmidt (March 7, 2022); 5.9 Contagions Worse Than COVID Will Prevail If Neglect of Global Public Health Continues by the Editors of *Scientific American* (March 1, 2022).

Each author biography was accurate at the time the article was originally published.

INDEX